GUARDING GABRIEL

J. A. WYNTERS

Guarding Gabriel

Editing by: Caitlin Fitzgerald

Cover design: Jo- Anne Walker

Interior Formatting: Dawn Lucous, Yours Truly Book Services

This book is dedicated to those who go to sleep clutching a book in their hands wishing their book boyfriends would step out and devour them.
Careful what you wish for.
It just might come true.

2005

"Why are you not real?" I scowled at my screen speaking to Gabriel.

"Why do you keep saying that?" he whispered in my ear as he snuck in behind me, his warm breath tickling my earlobe. I groaned at the prospect of him, my mouth watering.

I turned to him and grinned like the fool I was. He was melt worthy. Everything melted when he was around. My brain, my bones, my underwear. But of course, he was. That's how I designed him.

Gabriel was perfect. He was the husband I never had and the boyfriend I could never keep. I conjured him from pure air and he was just that, pure. He had a deep rumbling voice that turned to honey whenever he needed something from me. A frown that could turn water to ice, and a playful laugh, that swept you away. He had a chiselled jaw, with a permanent five o'clock shadow, that scratched in all the right places.

Liquid pools of chocolate brown eyes. The kind that pierced right through your clothes. The kind that told you exactly what he was thinking and in what position he was thinking of doing it.

He had untameable hair. Thick and lush. The kind that made your fingers twitch for just one touch. Mahogany brown, rich, deep, cut and styled but often I left it wild and unruly. I loved to gather it in my fist and curl my fingers against the thick locks.

He had the sort of lips that were full and soft. Ones that could possess you with a single kiss. They made me quiver. Not just when they were on me, but whenever he spoke.

Sometimes he was cruel, others coy, often he played hard to get, and sometimes I pretended like it was over just to feel the thrill of being chased. To watch his rippling chest, puff up when another suitor showed up. I loved the flare of his nostrils and the curl of his lips.

He wanted me to stay his.

He claimed me.

Just as I had wanted.

On occasion, I would push him aside. Watch him distraught as I dated another. He'd brood and sob and stalk the apartment until I took him back.

And when we made up…

I allowed him to take me in ways that took my mind to divine places. His powerful physique would clench and hold me. He would cage me in his arms as his large cock pumped into me furiously.

Filling me up.

Making me his.

Loving me.

God, I loved him. I loved his muscular arms and back covered in tattoos.

Gabriel.

The perfect man.

He was a God. An alpha, a biker, a billionaire, a broken cowboy and every woman's wet dream. Once he was even the owner of an exclusive BDSM club. That was a very fun time in my life.

Thing was. I had to share him. With millions of other women. I didn't resent him. I mean, I made him to be loved, cherished and coveted. And I knew that deep down, he was truly only mine. I created him. I breathed life into him and our affair was long and fruitful.

One doesn't become, and remain, a NYT bestselling author for a three-year stint without the perfect man.

Now I know you are rolling your eyes at me. How can he possibly be the perfect man?

Simple.

Because he was.

He cooked pasta in the nude and took me to Paris on his private jet, where he would send the air hostess away and go down on me for the duration of the flight. Of course, it's possible. He was a fictional character.

Well to most women he was. But to me, he grew as real as the desk I write at, or the pen I was holding, or the chair I was sitting on.

We were in love.

In lust.

In perpetual harmony. Except for the odd occasion. Because who really wants a man that doesn't call you on your shit and challenges your thoughts and actions?

We would argue about dialogue and how he would look. I'd give him a neck tattoo, and he'd argue that it would look better on his arm. We'd shout, he'd peel off his shirt and demonstrate. He'd be right. I'd grumble. He would grab my waist and kiss the back of my neck, softening my defeat.

It would happen with his clothes and hairstyle, the type of motorbike he rode and the jeans he wore. We once didn't speak for a month because I made him a millionaire instead of a billionaire. I mean what are a few zeros between lovers?

It was bliss.

A perfect existence of love and sex, and endless imagination and silly fights and hot naked nights.

Until.

I don't even know how to start this part of our story. It's so hard for me to write about something, someone - other than Gabe.

It was our first series, how it all started for us.

Gabriel.

His name is like prayer on my lips.

The move wasn't my idea. Gabriel suggested it after the third book of Guarding Gabriel hit the number one spot three days after its release. It remained at number one for 12 weeks. My publisher was laughing, and my bank account now competed with Gabriel's millions. I think his billionaire status was safe though.

We checked out the new high rise together. He found the apartment in a magazine. It belonged to some musician moving out of town, you know, one of those that suddenly needed to reconnect with nature or some such bullshit. Either way, the building was midtown and trendy.

Gabriel slid his fingers into mine as we rode the elevator to the 37th floor. We walked hand in hand as we looked over the five-bedroom apartment. It was an open plan design, modern in shades of white and grey.

We loved it.

I had a perfect city view from every angle, and my office would be a floating glass bubble above the world. We could tower over everyone. I'd put my desk in front of the giant glass window overlooking the park. It was going to be perfect.

The thing was, I could see us living there. I could see Gabe's naked ass as he cooked me a meal over the hotplate and I could see him having me for dessert over the kitchen island. The plush couch had more than enough room for the two of us, plus, did I mention the views? Well, they would take anyone's breath away.

I signed the contract for that apartment way too enthusiastically. Gabe kept telling me to keep my cool.

"Don't show so much interest. Play hard to get, let them chase you, I know you know how to play that game." He purred that last bit. He cleared his throat to add, "They will probably take 10k off the price. Stand your ground."

Of course, he was right, but I just waved him off. We loved the place. Why bother pretending we didn't? Sure, that 10k would have come in handy but I was in love with the image in my head, the life we would share, I didn't want to risk losing it all over 10k.

On the drive back home, he lowered my head onto his chest and brushed his fingers through my hair. It was a quiet ride even though I was bursting at the seams.

When the taxi dropped us off, he could smell how hungry I was for him. How I needed that celebration underneath him. He was ready, knowing just what I needed.

As the door shut behind me, he grabbed my waist and spun me around pinning me to the door. His kiss was warm and soft then hungry. His travelling hands found a way up my shirt and soon I was bare and wet and needy. I wrapped my legs around him and his hard cock slipped into me. He grunted like a beast, the low growl emanating from somewhere deep in his throat as he pounded against me, the wall thumping in his wake.

Those last three months in our old apartment were a blur of boxes and naked packing, coupled with some incredibly long and audible orgasms. I am pretty sure the neighbours had a big party when we left.

I would miss some of them though. Grish for example, he was always nice to me. Even before the fame and the money came. Especially before. We didn't see as much of one another as we did at the beginning, maybe cause all my time was occupied with Gabe, maybe because it made him uncomfortable hearing me having sex with someone that wasn't actually there. Either way, I went to have tea with him the day I left.

"So you're finally leaving us?" he said with the funny head dance he sometimes did.

"Yeah, I guess I am." I sipped the herbal tea he made. I never really liked it - I mean it was tea - but it would have been rude to refuse his offer.

"Where are you going?"

"Up town."

"Oooo fancy." His head shook to his whimsical voice.

I just giggled like a kid. He was like a dad giving me his stamp of approval and I can't lie I was happy to get it. It filled me up in a warm glow. I'm not sure why I always sought Grish's approval. Maybe because he'd always protected me, like a lion would their cub, fierce and tender, teaching me life lessons along the way. Maybe it was because he took me under his wing since that very first day.

The day I moved in it was pissing down with rain, because - why wouldn't it? My entire existence felt like it had just been flushed, so why not pile this shit on?

I had my worn backpack and a cardboard box. The box was slowly disintegrating in the rain and soon the very few possessions I had left would be piled on the street corner as pathetically as I was. Fat drops smacked my face as I stood looking up at the red brick building wishing I was inside. The building manager was meant to meet me there. Of course, he ran late. The awning above the entrance door to the building was rolled up, making it utterly useless. The taxi driver was reluctant to wait unless I paid him extra. I didn't have extra. When he mentioned he was prepared to accept other methods of payment I bailed.

So there I was, mascara running like snakes down my face, my clothes drenched and my box falling apart around the edges when he opened the door.

The man who walked through the door was wearing an orange dress. He would later tell me it was called a kurta. His jet-black hair peppered with grey, was combed perfectly to one side trying desperately to cover the obvious balding. His moustache was groomed and gleaming. I suspected it had enough oil in it to power a small motorbike.

I ran up to the door. With the backpack digging into my shoulders and my box heavy in my hands, I was too slow. The door closed behind the man with a muted click. The newcomer stood under a big black umbrella and we exchanged a brief look.

"Do you need help miss?"

I wasn't sure if I nodded before the tears came. The man gave me a pitiful look. The one you give a dog at a rescue shelter before you claim him as your own and take him home forever.

"The building manager is late..." I sniffed between heaving breaths, I could feel my lukewarm tears mix with the cold rain.

The man nodded. He dug into the folds of his perfectly, fitted kurta and dug out a small bunch of keys. They jingled against each other as he unlocked the door. He held it open for me and we stepped into the foyer.

I stood dripping. A puddle of water gathered around me. The man's eyes twitched as he stared at me intently, examining, calculating. I could see his mind working. He was probably wondering what to do with this stray he had picked up from the street. Could he trust me? Was I who I said I was? Could he leave me by myself?

I might have looked better if the rain hadn't ruined my hair and makeup. I could only guess that I looked like Alice Cooper having a very bad day. My clothes clung to me for dear life, they were probably ruined. Maybe not the worst thing. They were shit anyway. The long black skirt was old and stretched and since I hadn't eaten a proper meal in a few months was starting to slip off my hips, and not in a sexy way, but the - you need to eat something - way. The black singlet had a faded Van Halen album cover and a giant hole by the left armpit which I hid with my leather jacket. It belonged to Josh. Along with my heart and so much other stuff I just left behind.

Now that we were inside, I couldn't hide my shivering or my tears.

"What's your name miss?"

"Jane," I started and then felt the need to elaborate, just like I always do, which is why I guess I ended up where I did. "I'm meant to move into number 19 today, but the building manager just called and he's running late. He didn't leave me a key, and I had nowhere else to go…" I rattled off and Grish took a step back. He probably didn't want to get any crazy on his beautiful kurta.

He pulled out his phone from a hidden pocket in his kurta and put it to his ear. He spoke in Hindi, his voice remaining calm, though I could hear the person on the other end shouting. He did a good job pretending he couldn't hear them, then hung up and called a second number.

"Hello Barry?" he swayed his head as he talked. "This is Grish. I am taking the new girl to my apartment, when you come with her key, just knock on the door. She is soaking wet." I heard a mumble on the other end. "Well, then you should have told her sooner." His voice was stern, and that was the moment I knew things were going to get better.

When he finished, he put his phone away. "Come." He crossed the small entryway in three strides and pressed for the elevator. When the doors swung open, he held them open for me. This was a strange welcome to my new life.

We went up to the third floor, he shuffled into the dim corridor, the scratched old carpet lifting from the edges, frayed in places and worn to the concrete in others. I followed him in silence and stopped outside number 17. He pushed the door open, the smell of spice and incense hit me like a wall and once I recovered, I stepped into his apartment.

"Please take your shoes off and leave them by the door."

I did as he asked and waited. The box in my hands starting to feel like dead weight.

Grish disappeared behind a wall and came back a minute later with a towel in his hand. "You can put the box by the door too – dry yourself off and come to the kitchen. Straight through and on your left."

It seemed that somewhere between speaking to Barry and the elevator ride he made the decision to trust me, well, just long enough until Barry took me off his hands.

I put the box down, my hands cramping in agony. I peeled the soaking backpack from my back and placed it on top of the box.

Patting myself dry as best I could I looked around. The yellowing couch had the marks of a well-loved piece of furniture with a pronounced favourite side.

The orange curtains were partially opened and bathed the room in an orangey hue from the pale light leaking from outside.

A portrait of an elderly bearded man hung on his wall and the mantle held pictures of a stunning young woman and a younger version of the man who had shown me so much kindness. There were pictures of two kids also, a boy and a girl.

I took a few tentative steps and reached the kitchen. He was standing by a boiled kettle. Next to it stood a steaming teapot. He was busy pulling two cups from the light green kitchen cupboard above his head. It was a blindingly ugly colour, but I was grateful for anything other than that eye gouging orange.

He gestured to a chair pulled away from the oval table. I folded his towel in a semi-perfect square and sat on it knowing I would drench through it in a matter of minutes. If he suspected the same, he said nothing.

"I made tea." He smiled stiffly and placed the two cups on the table. He put the pot in the middle, then ruffled around in a cupboard and produced a tray of cookies. Most of which were gone. He looked at me sheepishly. I reached for one and shoved it down my throat. Whether it was my dishevelled appearance or the fact that I shovelled a second cookie too quickly I'll never know, but he pushed the tray closer to me and sat down.

He meticulously poured us each a cup and placed the teapot down.

He held the cup to his nose and sniffed the herbal infusion then took a short sip and put his cup back on the table.

"Jane, my name is Mr. Agrawal, but you can call me Grish."

"Thank you so much for your help. It's been a shit day." I immediately regretted my language as I saw the look in his eye. "Sorry." I grabbed my cup hoping to hide behind it. I brought it to my lips and sucked the drink.

It's harder than you think to keep a straight face while wanting to spew out a hot beverage from your mouth, whilst simultaneously holding the boiling cup of said beverage in your hand. I grimaced and eventually swallowed and explained quickly, "Too hot."

He just nodded, I'm not sure if he knew I was lying but if he did, he has been torturing me with his tea for the last three years and enjoying my suffering tremendously.

I tried finding my manners. I'm sure my deadbeat mom taught me a few before she disappeared. "You have a lovely home and a beautiful family. Where are your kids? Are they at school?"

"No, those are very old photographs." His lip curled ever so slightly to one side and I couldn't tell if it was a smile or a grimace. "Aadav, my boy, he just moved to New York City. The Big Apple." He beamed as he spoke. "He graduated from Harvard Law with honours and has been offered a job at a big firm."

"Congratulations." I raised my cup, but not to my mouth.

"Sona moved to Mumbai with her husband, almost three years ago now. She is expecting her second child in August." He was smiling again.

"You must miss them a lot."

"Yes."

"You and your wife must be excited to meet your new grandchild."

He gave me a melancholy look, one that said so much about youth being wasted on the young and how naïve we all are. He sighed a long, arduous sigh that was heartbreaking and comforting. "She's passed. About fifteen years ago now." He added as if to reassure me that the scar isn't as new, and the pain not as fresh. I knew, of course, he was putting a brave face on, and realised at once, that the picture display at the entrance was not just a display, but a shrine. If I had paid more attention, I would have noticed the orange flowers that stood in fresh water among the frames, and that there was not a speck of dust on any of the picture frames or counter on which they were laid.

I mumbled about how sorry I was and he brushed it off as something that's in the past. I let it go. If we were to be friends, I'd have enough time to ask him about it later.

"You look really nice. I hope you weren't going on a hot date." I probably should learn how to shut my mouth or at least finish a thought before saying it aloud.

He shook his head and sipped his tea. "Just a wedding. It's OK."

"Oh no, I'm so sorry. Look I can just wait in the foyer." I was already standing up and fumbling.

"Sit." He hadn't moved, but his voice was full of authority. He was definitely a dad.

"The wedding will take hours yet, days actually, and I have plenty of time. I have already spoken to my brother, and he is aware that I will be late. Barry will be here soon and you will get your keys and I can go then. Till then, get dry and drink your tea."

I grabbed the cup and sipped. The lukewarm water was green and swirls of wilted leaves swam casually on the bottom of the cup.

I forced myself to sip again and pondered what I could possibly ask this man that would not make for awkward or inappropriate conversation.

I was about to ask him what he did for a living when there was pounding at the front door.

"That must be Barry." His smile was cheerful and natural. He grabbed both teacups and placed them in the sink then pulled the plastic back over the two remaining cookies. He emptied the leaves from his teapot and set the rest next to the sink.

"Come Jane."

I stood up. The chair scraped the wooden floor beneath in a savage wail. I cringed. Grish didn't even turn around as he led me to the door.

"Barry." The name was clipped in his heavy accent, a high pitch reprimand.

"Sorry Grish," came a gruff voice from the other side of the door, "But you know how it is." There was a smirk behind the words and I decided just then that I hated Barry.

As if echoing my thoughts Grish started, "No Barry. I do not know how it is. You have a young lady waiting out in the rain and you are off canoodling with some stranger you probably met online, wasting everyone else's time."

Two thoughts occurred to me while Grish continued his tirade. I wasted his time, and I needed to find a way to show my gratitude. The second one was how is it that the building manager was getting laid at 11 a.m. on a Saturday morning. I slid into my shoes, slipped my backpack on and grabbed my box. I turned to Grish who was heaving.

"Can I help you with your box, Jane?" he offered.

"No, thank you erm … Mr. Agrawal … I've taken far too much of your time this morning."

He considered my words and perhaps his. "Not at all, it was nice to meet you." He gave me a cheerful smile that made me believe he meant it.

"Barry! Come take this young lady's box."

"No, it's OK…" My words dropped almost as low as my jaw.

His emerald green eyes flicked over my body; his face down-turned as if I was a total disappointment. He yanked my box in his muscular arms and turned to Grish. He seemed sheepish when he apologised for a final time. Grish huffed and walked toward the elevator while I followed Barry across the hall and two doors down.

"Here you go, number 19."

"Jane."

"Sure."

He unlocked the door and stepped inside discarding my box on the green couch along the wall and waved at the room.

"Living area here, kitchen this way." He pointed to his right where the tiny kitchen lived. "Your bedroom and toilet through there." He pointed toward the dark corridor. "Rubbish collection on Thursdays. I am also the maintenance guy for his building, so if you have any issues, here's my number."

He finally turned around, and I got another look at his beautiful features. His golden locks squared his perfect face. Hair growth peppered his chiselled jaw and his drenched, white shirt clung to his torso. I could see every muscle as it rippled under the shirt. I wondered what it would feel like to bite into that flesh. I'd probably break all my teeth. It would be like biting into concrete. I shook the thought from my head and reached for the card. He might be pretty, but he was an inconsiderate asshole.

"Are you going to apologise?" I snatched the card from his hand.

"No." He turned towards the door.

I searched my brain for a witty, smart, angry retort, but as I opened my mouth only breath came out. I could possibly interpret it as an adoring sigh as I watched his jean-clad ass sashay out of my apartment.

"Call me if you have any maintenance issues." He was already walking down the hall. "And don't be late with rent."

Rent. Shit. That would be tomorrow's problem.

I kicked the door shut and sighed. I was home. In a home, that was mine. Safe. Alone.

Alone.

I studied the living area. The green couch came with the place as did the fridge. I'd have to work out a bed arrangement but that would have to wait. I looked at the bare walls and imagined where I could put a TV if I ever got one, and where I could put a pot plant - a plastic one obviously - because I could never keep anything alive. Not really.

I took the two steps to the kitchen. A mantle against the wall with a built-in sink and a hot plate. Cupboards that were built in the 50s and painted cruelly in the 70s. I'd have to remember to wear sunglasses every time I entered the room.

I walked down the corridor and found two doors. One was my bedroom. An empty white room. Four walls and wooden skirtings. A window stood slightly ajar, looking out onto the red brick building next door.

The bathroom was my last stop.

And I kind of wish I had never gone inside, or gone inside far sooner. The scariest thing in that bathroom, apart from the screaming yellow bathtub, was me.

My hair was plastered to my face. Curly wisps which escaped my bun and managed to dry stood in a frenzy like a frizzy crown above my head. What lipstick I had, vanished along with my pride as I realised two people had seen me like this.

I sighed and pretended I didn't suddenly wish Barry was an old fat man.

I slung my backpack off my back, letting it fall with a thud onto the tiles. One by one I peeled the clothes off me, damp and clammy, they felt like I was peeling a second skin.

Shedding.

And maybe I was.

I rummaged around my backpack hoping for something dry among the damp collection of clothes. I found some granny underwear and an oversized t-shirt somewhere in the centre of the bag.

Goodbye old life.

Hello granny underwear.

The shower was warm and relief flooded through me. Something worked. I wouldn't have to call Barry and let him see me in my granny underwear.

I got dressed and spent a considerable amount of time strategically hanging clothes across various surfaces in the hopes they would eventually dry.

I opened my box and pulled out what was effectively my kitchen.

One kettle, a jar of coffee, a jar of sugar, and a few packs of two-minute noodles. Of course, they came with an array of plastic cups and dishes. I also pulled out the purple tie-dye sheet praying it would dry by bedtime.

I sucked my sloppy noodles while scrolling through my phone. I highlighted seven potential jobs in case the one that Scott set up for me fell through.

Ah, Scott.

There is a lot to say about Scott, but I won't. All I'll say was that his heart was as fiery as his red hair and I owed him a lot. He knew it. But he'd never mention it or ask for anything in return, for which I was eternally grateful cause I knew exactly how he wanted me to repay his favours. But to be honest, sitting for hours on Xbox, and teaming up against some French guys who probably still lived in their parent's basement, was not my idea of fun.

The apartment became darker, night closed in. I fell asleep somewhere between barista and waitress.

Riveting stuff.

When I woke up my face was lying in a damp pool of spittle and my neck hurt from being twisted in what was an unnatural position for at least eight hours.

The apartment felt cold. Lifeless. It was probably an open window, but it felt a lot like my life.

When I realised tapping on the door was what woke me, I froze. The knocking, soft but insistent.

"Coming," I garbled. I felt as if a turkey had died in my mouth and was attempting some kind of resurrection.

I should have looked through the peephole, but I didn't.

"You shouldn't just open your door like that." Grish's severe face curled in a scowl.

I frowned at him but it was more of an effort to keep my eyes open, body upright and brain firing on all cylinders.

I said nothing. I stood there swaying like a reed and wiped my mouth. He, on the other hand, was meticulously groomed, not a hair out of place, on his head or face. He wore a red kurta adorned with golden lace, pressed into perfectly firm lines.

"What time is it?"

"Eight in the morning." It was hard for me to infer what he wanted with his tone. But it felt something like a reproach. Adults should be awake and dressed and ready for a full day of adulting. I was way behind.

"Would you like to come in?" the sentence was out of my mouth before my brain could stop it.

"Thank you." He took a step inside and I could see his effort at hiding his horror, or was it disgust?

"Are the rest of your things arriving today?"

I grimaced and my eyes swept the room.

"No."

"You don't have much." It wasn't a question. All he had to do was take one look at the room strewn with drying clothes and my sad little couch to realise that was all I owned.

"Coffee?"

"I only drink tea."

"Sorry I don't have any."

"It's OK"

It didn't feel OK.

He followed me to the kitchen and his eyes roamed the room. He watched me closely as I made a coffee and poured the steaming hot water into my plastic cup.

I could swear he shook his head but said nothing.

"I noticed yesterday you didn't have much with you, so I brought you some food from the wedding. Moving is hard work."

For the first time, I noticed the small tub in his hands.

He placed it on the mantle and opened the lid. Immediately the small space filled with the most delectable aromas and my stomach sang its morning song asking for nourishment.

"Thank you." I meant it but I hesitated before approaching. I don't know why I felt like I needed permission.

"Please, go ahead."

I grabbed the box and lifted the paper towel that held my salvation.

"Aloo tikki," he said as I examined the round fried potato cakes.

I ate in silence letting myself enjoy a meal that wasn't noodles. I ate two cakes and decided to leave the other two for lunch.

My stomach gurgled with pain and resentment.

"There is more."

I dug out the wrapped parcel to discover a second placed below.

I unwrapped it and found flatbread and between the two slices, I could see a thick brown layer of chocolate and what could have only been strawberries.

I gawked at the bread.

"The naan was plain. My daughter always used to complain about it so I used to spread the chocolate and cut the strawberries for her, sometimes she liked banana or almond but I wasn't sure…"

Suddenly this beautiful and generous man seemed sheepish.

"No, I love it. All."

I grabbed the food and let my stomach sing as it revelled in the sweetness that was my breakfast.

I took out the rest and placed it on the empty shelf of my fridge. I sipped my coffee and felt like a human again.

"Can I use your bathroom please?"

"The door to the right."

He turned and walked down the corridor navigating through the trails of clothes and random items that I somehow managed to hold on to.

When he came back, I was taking the last sip of coffee.

"You don't have a bed." It was a statement and once again it felt like he was judging my ability to adult.

"No." It came out almost as an apology. I was going for matter of fact. I made a mental note to practice my tone when speaking to people.

"I need to go."

"Oh."

"The wedding…"

"Of course. Thank you, Mr. Agrawal."

"Call me Grish." He gave me what could only be described as a grim smile and left.

Despite the food in my belly and the coffee, his sudden departure left me empty again.

I sighed and pushed away from the door. There would be plenty of time for lamenting later – right then, I needed to get ready for my job interview.

My shirt was too tight and my skirt too short but that's how I was told to dress. Was I comfortable? No. Was I broke? Definitely! Sometimes we do what we must.

I splashed some colour on my face and coated my lips with Fire Breather red lipstick.

Scott's brother was his opposite, in every way. Whereas Scott was what one might label a nerd with lanky, unruly hair that covered up a pimply face, and pale flesh from the unhealthy obsession with playing video games. Leon was the kind of guy girls tripped over. Or more often pushed each other out of the way for.

I'm fairly sure he was taller, but that's because I don't really remember what Scott looked like standing up. Leon's shoulders sloped over swollen muscles that rippled under his tight shirts and tighter suit pants. He was always clean shaven, his nails were perfectly manicured, and his hair brushed in a wave to the left. It accentuated his carved jaw that was always in motion. Talking, clenching, sucking, kissing.

It was hard to stand still and not fall on to your back and

spread your legs every time you were in the room with the guy. He had beautiful thick lips, ones that you knew you could bite, ones that you knew could play havoc with anything they touched.

He gave me a flicker of a smile as I walked in. His office was as plush as he was. Neat and tidy and perfectly beautiful. Every piece of furniture flawlessly placed, each item of decor adding just the right touch to complete the room and every surface meticulously clean.

He waved to the single chair that was set in front of his broad desk, and nodded, acknowledging my presence. I sat quietly watching him listen to the phone he held to his ear. Watching him watch me. Watching his eyes lazily trail the line of my boots up to my knees and follow the line of my stockings up my thighs. When he hesitated there, I begged my underwear to refrain from exploding. He continued his journey again, pausing at the swell of my breasts as they peaked beyond my shirt. He bit his lip, and I almost slipped off my chair.

I inhaled trying to settle my hammering heart.

As he said his goodbyes, his scorching brown eyes landed on my lips. I bit my tongue, the desire to lick my suddenly dry lips urgent. I squirmed in my chair as he set his phone on the desk.

"You must be Jane." His voice was as dangerous as he was. It offered promises while being completely casual.

"Yes, hi." I commended myself on managing to stay cool.

I wasn't.

"Scott was holding out, wasn't he?" his eyes seemed to darken.

I stayed silent. What sort of question was that?

"Can you wait tables?"

"Yes."

"Do you have more outfits like that one?"

"Yes."

"Can you start tonight?"

I almost jumped out of my seat. Panic. Excitement. Pleasure. I wasn't prepared for this interview to go quite like this. "You don't want to test me or anything?"

Leon stood up his lip curled in a wicked smile. He pushed his chair back as he stood up, his jacket hung over the back. His muscles rippled through the tailored button-up shirt with each predatory step he took toward me.

"Do you know what we sell here, Jane?" his voice was soft, an undercurrent of something dangerous lay beneath.

"Alcohol? Bar food?" I offered meekly as I began to hyperventilate under his unnerving stare.

His eyes remained locked on mine as he closed the distance between us, taking measured slow steps.

"No."

"No?"

He came to a complete stop squaring his body before my chair then leaned back casually against his desk, his hands clutching the rim.

"No, Jane." The way he said my name sent shivers down my spine.

He took the two steps that separated us and leaned over me, his hot breath on my ear, his spiced cologne intoxicating me.

I needed to remember how to breathe. His body inches from mine, hovered in the charged space between us. I shifted in the chair. He shifted an inch so that his face was a hairsbreadth from mine. His long delicate fingers found their way to my knee, light feather touch, just enough to know they were there.

I swallowed, my mouth a desert, I knew could be quenched by his. He traced his hands slowly up my thigh as he made a guttural purr. His eyes never leaving mine.

He clenched his jaw his face tightening and pulled away.

"We sell sex, Jane."

"Sex? That's not what Scott said…" Suddenly the heat seeped away from my body and all I wanted to do was run.

"Not sex-sex." He grunted and moved away from me. "The idea of sex. And you Jane," he grunted to himself, "You have a look about you Jane. A look I have been looking for. A look I need around here."

When I continued to sit in silence nibbling the inside of my lip, Leon continued.

"Our clientele are what you might call horn dogs. They are young, spoilt and privileged. They think they can own everything and everybody. The women who work here are unattainable. They cannot be touched or bought or owned. It drives them crazy. They come here to compete. To see who will break first. To see what money can and can't buy."

I nodded absorbing what he was saying.

"If you work here, you are to dress provocatively. Tease them. The more they want you the more tips you will earn. Is it derogatory? Yes, but it makes us both money. If you walk out of here with any of my paying customers do not come back. If I hear you have taken money for services other than the service of alcohol, your job here will be terminated. If you allow any of these men to touch you or treat you other than you deserve, you will not be welcome here. Do you understand?"

I nodded wondering if leaning into me was how I deserved to be treated. He retreated back to his desk and was leaning against it once more.

"You will work five days a week and most weekends. You will be paid weekly and you can keep all the tips that you earn. Your shifts are seven hours long and include all your meals."

He stared at me, his eyes burning holes through my clothes, undressing me as I sat across from him. Is this what all his paying patrons would do?

"Do you have any questions?"

"What did you mean about Scott?"

He chuckled at my question. "I just told you that you will be getting paid for horny men to leer at you all day long. You will serve them and they will objectify you as the thing of their dirty dreams and you want me to talk about my brother?"

"Yes." I twisted in my chair again and wondered if I would ever be able to wear my underwear again. The amount of moisture down there would have disintegrated the fabric by now.

He ran a hand through his hair and smoothed out locks that were placed exactly where they needed to be.

"Well, look at you," he cleared his throat. "He told me about you five years ago, said you looked good. But good doesn't really cover it does it, Jane? See, I thought I was going to meet a mousy little girl. Someone that's not used to any kind of attention. Someone my brother might find… more attainable." He waved his hand as if trying to conjure a picture in mid-air. "Someone who shares his hobbies, you know?"

"Scott is a good guy." I crossed my arms.

"He is."

"He is my friend." I raised my voice at his nonchalant attitude.

"That's why I was doing him this favour. I wasn't really intending on hiring anyone today." Heat flushed to my face.

"He's a good guy."

"You said that already." His lip curled, and he stood up making his way to a drink tray tucked near a bookshelf kissing the window. The ice clinked in the tumbler as he threw a few cubes into it and topped it with amber liquid.

"I have other prospects."

"Do you?" he turned around and took a quick sip from his drink. "Tell me?" he made his way back to his desk and leaned against it. The clear shape of his erection pushed against his tailored suit pants.

"I am…" I cleared my throat ungluing my eyes from the bulge. "A barista… at the coffee shop down the street."

"That position is no longer available."

"How do you know?"

"Louis, down at the coffee shop? He works for me. I will tell him that if he hires you, he will lose his job."

"Why?" I launched myself out of the chair, my jaw clenching.

"Because I want you." It was a gruff guttural sound. "To work for *me*." He covered up. "You can earn a lot more here than you will anywhere else in the neighbourhood."

"What if I don't want to be objectified?"

"Jane." There he was with my name again. "You know as well as I do that wherever you go, men look at you with a special kind of attention. Why not get paid for it?" his knuckles were white as he clutched onto the lip of the desk.

"Can I start tomorrow? I need to buy some food. I moved to a new place yesterday."

"You start tonight. Food will be provided."

"What about breakfast tomorrow morning?"

"Don't make me answer that the way that I want to."

The interview was over.

This was something else.

I took a step in his direction, I was so close his cologne enveloped me.

He didn't move, didn't flinch.

His eyes remained on mine. His jaw locked.

"I'm still going to need breakfast tomorrow." I stepped closer on wobbly feet, my body grazed his. I could feel his erection flinch in his pants.

At that, his demeanour changed, and he sidestepped around me then turned towards the big window overlooking the street.

"You are off limits."

"Says who?"

He didn't answer. He didn't need to.

Scott.

"Also, I don't sleep with my staff."

My heart which had been doing somersaults in my throat stopped mid flip and dropped like lead back to my chest where it shrivelled and cowered away.

"So what was all that before?"

"Me being stupid. I am sorry It will never happen again. Consider me one of your customers. I am off limits. If you touch me again, you will be fired." His tone had turned dry and cold. "Be here at seven and ask for Sammy. She'll show you the ropes. Do not be late."

He turned back to the window with a tone of finality and the most bizarre interview I had ever had, came to an abrupt end.

But at least I had a job.

G abriel grabbed me by the waist and landed one of his devastating kisses on me. His towering height always made me feel safe, and his broad shoulders caged around me as he held me in a protective and warm embrace.

We had spent most of the day unpacking, the boxes littering the floor thinned out into smaller piles of books and stuff.

Stuff.

I had so much stuff.

That hungry wet girl from two years ago adulted and turned shit around.

"You're distracting me, I need to finish unpacking." I tried to move away from him but Gabriel grabbed my neck and started massaging that aching spot that sits permanently between my neck and shoulder blades. I sighed.

"You've been working too hard Jane. Let me make you some coffee, maybe dinner?"

"Coffee and take away. What should we have?"

"Korean?"

"You read my mind."

"I always do." I felt the softness of his lips on my neck as he released his grip on me.

"We are going to love it here."

"Yes. We. Are."

I picked up the phone and ordered Korean wondering what Grish would be having for dinner and hoping the new tenant would be a better one than I was. Or with more than a backpack and a soggy box of belongings to their name.

Everything here was so modern. So meticulous.

I shivered.

This was a lot like Leon's office. I could feel Gabriel frowning behind me at the mention of his name.

"He's gone. You don't have to worry about him anymore. It's just you and me Gabe babe."

"I hate when you call me that."

"No, you don't."

He mock pouted and sat on the couch grabbing a book from the top of a pile and flipping through it. He wasn't reading, just scanning the pages indiscriminately.

I loved watching him like that. Just being. Breathing. Existing.

Shirtless. (I don't remember him taking his shirt off, but he's unforgettable with a bare torso and wicked grin.) He leaned back, his tanned complexion stark against the cream couch. His chiselled abs on display like corrugated iron, defined in clear beautiful furrows, trailed by thick black hair from his belly and disappearing somewhere under his belt. He wore my favourite pair of jeans. The ones that stuck to his ass and fell off his hips around the narrow shape of his waist.

He was pretending not to notice me. Ignoring me like I wasn't stalking the room, prowling towards him like a hungry predator.

"I thought you were hungry," he said when I straddled him, his eyes smouldering.

"I am." I grabbed the book from his hand and threw it on the coffee table, then pressed my lips to his. Always inviting. Always soft. Always perfect.

He kissed me just how I needed him to, wild and hungry. Desire spilt from him, saturating the room. I could feel him grow harder beneath me. The undulated movement of my hips spurring him on.

"You've had a big day." His breath stalled in his throat. "Let me help you relax."

In a swift movement, I was on my back, sinking into the cool leather. The lights blazing above my head silhouetting his flawless face. He trailed kisses down my neck and along my collarbone. He slipped the straps of my singlet and bra off and kissed my shoulders, then made his way to the other side. Slow and steady. Easing me into his game.

He slid my singlet down taking my bra with it trapping my hands in the straps.

"Exquisite," he breathed then grabbed a nipple between his teeth biting ever so softly.

I groaned for him, arching my back, wanting him to take more of me. Faster. Harder.

He ignored my silent pleas and took his time. kissing, licking and biting my nipple while pinching and pulling on the other.

"Please."

"Shhhhh. Don't rush me."

He swapped over, my nipples ripe and ready, hard and wet. The cool air playing havoc with his warm breath.

"So pretty. So eager."

His mouth found mine, and he quenched my need momentarily. Gabriel's hands followed the groove of my belly, along the shape of my hips and inserted fingers into the elastic of my pants. He dragged, releasing me slowly from the fabric.

"Magnificent." Gabriel licked his lips as his eyes studied

my exposed body. Parting my thighs, he forced my knees apart. He laid kisses on my inner thigh, his whiskers scratched my skin, leaving an echo of his presence.

When his tongue found me, I was so needy. I could feel his smile as I moaned. My pulse hammered through my veins as his tongue swirled and teased, devastatingly slowly, agonisingly blissful, unbearably bearable. Soft and slow, hard and fast.

"Please," I begged him for a second time.

Gabriel pulled away a smile tugged at his glistening lips. "Whatever you want Jane."

"I want you inside me."

His face rose from between my legs and I could hear his zipper opening. The jeans fell away to reveal his hard cock straining against his boxers. He pulled them off and let me have a long lingering look at his beautiful cock, the pulsing, the veins, the eager twitching.

His weight landed on me as his head found my opening, and with a low guttural groan he was inside me. Measured and considered. Each thrust getting me closer, leaching the orgasm from my body, wreaking havoc on all my systems. He ground against me, his hips increasing speed, desperate, possessive, needy.

Gabriel's hands found my breasts and his mouth mine as he pounded against me pushing me over the edge. I exploded in pleasure, every synapse alight, my body shivering with delight sinking in his pheromones.

I lay beneath him panting. The air scented by sex and sweat. I sucked in breath regaining some semblance of 'normality.' It was just how I had imagined it. Just what I needed it to be.

I lay with my head buried in his chest listening to the rhythm of his heart as it settled. The beat slowing to a calm thump. I loved those moments. The quiet after the storm, the feel of him above me, the *knowing* he was there. My fingers curled around his little trail of hair, pulling releasing, teasing.

It might have ended differently had the doorman not rang.

"Hello? Miss Miller?"

"Yes?" Still breathless.

"There's a delivery man downstairs can I send him up?"

"Sure thing, thank you…?"

"Rob." I could hear him smile over the phone.

"Thank you, Rob." I smiled back and hung up.

I was now living in one of those buildings that provided fair warning before anyone could come up and interrupt. There would be no more surprise visits. The prospect was both satisfying and depressing.

"Our dinner is here."

"I think I filled up on dessert." Gabriel smirked at me from the couch. His body moulded in the leather, his nakedness on full display.

I swallowed hard. "Oh, shut up."

Gabriel snickered like a teenager. "Best pull yourself together Jane." He winked at me and I caught my reflection in one of the large dark windows that now surrounded my apartment. My wild hair stood in a tangled mess and my clothes were sitting at all the wrong angles. I grabbed a hair tie and looped my hair into a bun. Then adjusted my pants and shirt.

The knock on the door was harsh and rapid.

"Yes. Yes, I am coming." I grabbed my wallet and exchanged a few pleasantries with the delivery boy. He was young and tall, and in a hurry. But he gave me a knowing look, one that said he knew exactly what I just did. It was in the twitch of his lips and the flare of his nose. In the step he took to be closer to me, and his pupils growing bigger in his young horny eyes. I paid him and closed the door.

Gabriel was staring at me.

"What?"

"He was perving."

"So?" I shrugged and took the food to the kitchen and placed it on the island.

Gabriel pushed himself off the couch. The flush of physical activity turned to that of anger.

"So?" he closed the distance between us his body crashing against mine pinning me to the cold marble surface.

"Gabriel."

"You're mine Jane." His nose flared as he landed a possessive kiss on my lips his mouth devouring me.

"I'll always be yours Gabe." I breathed softly to him and he released me.

"I don't like sharing you."

"I know." I traced my fingers along his face. "And tonight, you don't have to." I gave him an appeasing smile hoping to put the matter at rest. I pulled out a plate and reached to grab my food when I felt him behind me. His fingers sank into my pants seeking me out. Reminding me who I belonged to.

"Gabriel," I whispered as he leaned over me. His strong body pinning me to the cold marble as he stroked and swirled his fingers expertly.

"You're mine, Jane." His skilled fingers moved faster, circling, stroking, gliding.

My hips moved against him, grinding against his fingers in a feverish pace, needing release. "I'm yours," I whispered as I moaned into the kitchen counter. "Don't stop, I'm so close."

He pulled his fingers away and pulled my pants down I could feel his hardness against me.

"Say it again Jane. Say it again and I'll let you cum."

"I'm yours, Gabriel."

With that, he was inside me. Buried deep. My name fell off his lips in a muted groan. His fingers returned and his hips began to move faster as he pumped against me. Bringing me to the edge.

"Gabriel, I'm..." My legs twitched beneath him as I exploded. My hands grasping at the ridged stone, aching for his body. He continued to pump, his pace quickening his breath halted as I felt the tremble of his release inside me. He pulled me to him sinking deeper, savouring my warmth.

When we settled, he kissed my shoulder gently then purred in my ear, "Mine."

Still overwhelmed with sensation, I nodded. Gabriel released me, lifting his body and turning away.

I heard the door to the bathroom slam shut as I peeled myself from the counter and pulled up my pants which were still at my knees.

He had been jealous before. But today was new. Today was angry and needy, possessive and bitter.

I would have to do something about Gabriel.

I didn't bother changing the outfit I wore for my interview. It was already showing all leg and most of my boobs so there was no point. I also noticed how affected Leon was by it. The thought of him sent a small shiver down to my core. I shook it off as I entered the bar.

It was different from what I had imagined it to be. I thought it would be one of those dark places with plush red walls and dimmed lights. Instead, it was another version of Leon's office. I wondered if this is what the inside of Leon would look like if you had to pry him open.

Everything was pristine and sophisticated. A long marble counter stretched across the well-lit bar. Too well-lit if you asked me. When you go drinking the lights should be dim. It helps you make more mistakes you can regret later, and the alcohol seems to daze your senses faster.

There was room for a live band at the far end, and tables with stools were scattered across the floor space that wasn't reserved for dancing. It was clear that no expense was spared. I bet that if I sold one of those stools, I would be able to pay my rent for three months.

I was intrigued and fascinated and a little disappointed.

A tall, stunning blonde with eyes that made your clothes explode off your body on their own volition, walked towards me. I bet she was his biggest money maker. She stretched out a perfectly manicured hand and shook mine. "Sammy." She gave me a bright and beautiful smile. Perfectly white straight teeth like she'd just walked off the set of a teeth whitening commercial.

I wondered if she and Leon got their manicures together. "Jane."

"Welcome to The Hot Bird." She gave me a once over and nodded. "I see what he means."

I didn't know if she was talking to me or herself so I kept quiet.

"Let me show you what we do around here." She winked at me and turned around gesturing with her finger to follow.

She made it look so sexy. Later, I would stand in front of a mirror and try. Try to get that look in my eye. Try to get my single digit to produce saliva and desire in the same way I saw her doing all night. I would fail. But at least I tried.

I followed her, my eyes flicking from her golden curls that jumped on her head like a million charged slinkies, and her glorious ass that was wrapped in a body-hugging leather mini skirt. Her underwear was a hairsbreadth away from any object at any time. Showing it off, teasing the customers with peeks. A thrill igniting whatever their imagination, because she knew it would remain untouched. Every time she bent over, I could see the sliver of her red G-string. She was attractive in all the right places and I was simultaneously jealous and totally in awe.

Sammy led me through a hidden door that led down a narrow corridor. She showed me the staff toilet and change room, and the locker where I could keep my bag and extra clothes which she said I should bring from now on. She said if no one "accidentally spilt" a drink on me all night to see if my nipples would harden under the cold liquid, I wasn't going to last very long. I swallowed hard and wondered if that's why she wore the tight white singlet and red lacy bra.

When I asked her about Leon's speech and how we should be treated she smirked at me.

"He meant every word, but the girls told him to back off when he stopped it from happening."

My heart flared, he was a good guy. "So, you want to have drinks thrown at you?"

"Want is a strong word." She scrunched her face as we retraced our steps back towards the main room. "I don't *want* to have drinks thrown at me, but I do want to earn a living. See, I am this close to paying off my house." She held her thumb and forefinger inches apart. "Even though I've asked him to stop, Leon has been putting some money away for me, so that when I own my house, I can go study. Hard nipples will get you triple your tips. The guys won't touch you, but they will splash you."

She giggled at her little rhyme and pushed through the door that led us back onto the main room. I could feel my body stiffen, the hair on my neck doing a Mexican wave. I wondered about Leon and Sammy.

While doing a quick tour of the bar her voice became muted, swallowed by the uncertainty in my head. If they were having a relationship what about the fireworks in his office earlier that day? When I tuned back in, she was showing me the band space, dance floor, tables and outside area. I tried to keep up. When was it too soon to ask your manager if they were sleeping with your boss?

At around eight thirty, two large tall men walked in. They were clad in black suits and silky black ties and looked like they were forged from a mountain. Solid and strong.

"Hi boys." Sammy smiled at them and I could instantly see their affection for her as their faces softened, quaint smiles at the top of their lips. There wasn't a trace of lust or desire, but a bond. A friendship, like they would do anything for her.

"This is Jane, the new girl. That's Dave and Lefty, they will make sure you're always safe." Her smile widened, and they turned their attention to me.

"Hi." I extended my hand. Dave was the first to grab it in his paw. He gave me a big grin and chimed his hello in a deep baritone. Lefty followed.

Sammy reached behind the bar and handed them each a cool bottle of water which they took as they bid us a good night and went to set up for their own night.

"They don't say much, do they?"

"They know their place and they want to keep their jobs. Also, they're not really into girls…"

Before I could react, she took my hand and pulled me behind the bar. We went through fridges and recipes. Alcohol contents and where they kept the cherries and lemon slices. She must have seen the dazed look on my face as she stopped talking and put a reassuring hand on my forearm.

"I know it's a lot to take in, but remember this, these men, they come here to drink, yes, but they also come here to watch you make their drink. If it takes you five minutes instead of two, they get their money's worth. They get to stare at your ass or your tight stomach or your neck or whatever little thing they will fantasise about later. Take your time. Learn. Don't be flustered." She squeezed. "You will learn fast and you will learn better on the job. It pays well and you, my dear, have a lot of assets." Her face broke into her practised smile that beamed at me.

I hoped she was right.

That first night was a blur of music and alcohol and a lot of hands. I would get better at swatting them away or avoiding them all together, but that night, I was touched in places I didn't even know men wanted to touch.

Sammy was right. I had three drinks thrown at me and she gave me two spare outfits. The last one, a white singlet cut along the midriff exposing my belly, tied in a little knot just above my navel. The sleeves were torn off. I wasn't sure if it was designer, or designed by Sammy, but it got me more attention than I had anticipated, and yet another drink "spilt" across my chest. Seemed Leon had very clumsy clientele.

I was out of clothes and out of luck. I reeked of alcohol and my nipples stood like soldiers saluting their general. I was leered at and propositioned, enticed and stared at, but most of all I made money. A shit ton of money. Enough money to buy food, for two weeks, maybe three if I stretched it out.

Leon wasn't lying. He sold sex. And I sold my soul. But I needed to eat and keep a roof over my head. Basic survival.

The only other thing I remember from that night is when I first saw him. Leon showed up downstairs around midnight. It wasn't long after my last change and I felt his eyes bore into me as he sat at the end of the bar conversing with a group of patrons.

Leon wore a charcoal grey suit that wrapped around his body like glad wrap showing every inch of muscle and anatomy that lay beneath. His perfectly combed hair glistened under the bar lights and his eyes burned as he stared at me, following my every move. I gave him a small smile and pretended that my underwear was still intact under his gaze as I casually turned down suitors and collected empty glasses.

When I reached the bar to empty my tray, he came up behind me. His large frame blocked out the glaring light above my head and I could feel the heat of his body as he inched closer.

"How are you finding your first night?" his voice rolled through me.

"Busy."

"I can see that."

I grabbed the empty glasses and bent down to place them

into the dishwasher. My ass brushed his groin, and I felt his erection against me. I froze. He sucked in a long breath but didn't move. Neither did I. I stood up again, then repeated the action. I thought I could hear him groan over the music and the loud chatter, but that might have been my imagination.

I could feel his hard cock as it stood straining against his charcoal pants. I could feel how he wanted me. Everything tingled. My heart hammered in my chest as I continued this one-sided dance. Leon didn't move an inch as I packed up the entire dishwasher and set it to wash. As soon as I pushed the start cycle button, he took two steps back and left the bar. I didn't see him again that night.

$\sim$

It was edging on 3 a.m. when I got home. I reeked of booze and cologne and sweat and lust. My first night at The Hot Bird was done, and I was exhausted, exhilarated and highly confused.

I stacked the dollar notes under my couch pillow.

I peeled off my sticky shirt. Sammy's purple bra stuck to my body, and I threw it on the floor. I took off the borrowed skirt and boots and got under the hot shower. The water pelted my skin. My body felt exhausted and abused in ways it hadn't been in years. My feet hurt, my thighs hurt, my head screamed and all I could think about was Leon's cock and how he had stood there, just letting my ass sway and bend against it.

The thought made me angry. Hungry. For him. I closed my eyes and envisioned Leon. Imagined his big hands around my nipples, pinching rolling, touching. I imagined his big cock inside me, the hardness filling me as he pushed into me, bending me over the dishwasher. Taking me right there in the bar. Everyone to watch, to see my face contort in ecstasy as he fucked me, sucked me, finished me. I came in throbbing pulsing mess my back stuck to the wall, my legs barely holding up my own weight.

I slipped into the first thing I found that was close and dry and crashed on the couch.

~

There it was again. That rapping sound like someone was tapping in my head. I rolled over and groaned. The sound continued, and I opened my eyes. The morning sun still soft. It was early, too early. Why the hell was someone knocking at my door?

I swung it open and immediately jumped behind it, realising I was not properly dressed for what awaited me on the other side.

"Good morning," Grish mumbled visibly embarrassed.

"Hi Grish. Sorry, it was a late night. I got a job."

"Congratulations." He flashed some teeth and his mouth returned to its parental status quo hovering between concern and judgement. "I have something for you." He gestured as if I hadn't seen what he brought.

"I'll just go put some more clothes on." He nodded as I closed the door in his face. I could feel the heat rising up to my ears as I ran around the apartment picking up my now dry clothes. I threw them on the couch pretending they were in a neat pile. I cringed and shook it off. I found short jeans and a t-shirt that covered my shoulders. I grabbed my hair and put it up in a bun and splashed some water on my face.

I opened the door again.

Grish was talking to the other young men. When he saw me, he exchanged a few words in Hindi and the men grabbed the wooden planks and some tools and went directly down the corridor and into my bedroom.

"Grish, you shouldn't have."

He put his hands up in a gesture that made me think I had offended him.

"Thank you."

To that, he smiled a little. "My daughter doesn't need it anymore. Even if they come to visit, they will stay in a hotel room." He sighed. "Anyway, no young lady should be sleeping on a couch at night. Do you have blankets?"

I eyed my lightweight sheet. The stark purple tie-dye drowned out the ugliness of the couch.

Grish didn't say anything else about it.

A few minutes later the men came back. They seemed to be joking, all talking at once. They quieted down when they saw Grish.

"Uncle, we are done." The man was young, maybe in his early twenties. His accent was thick and wrapped in spice and adventure.

"Grab the mattress," Grish said and the two younger men exited and came back with a mattress I had not noticed before. I guessed it must have been leaning on the wall.

In two minutes, the boys were back again and Grish dismissed them.

"Thank you," I called to them as they disappeared down the hall. "Thank you Grish. Truly."

I wanted to hug him. I didn't. We weren't there yet.

"Wait here." He left, and I ran to my bedroom. The single bed had been built and placed under the window. Old ornate wood with hand carved swirling designs ran along the edges. It was the most beautiful thing I had ever been given.

"Jane?" Grish's voice boomed down the corridor and I popped my head out to see him by the door. "I told you to stay here, anyone could have come in." He was back to admonishing. His forehead crinkled. I bit my lip holding back a smile. It's like he really cared.

He was holding a thick duvet and pillow, both covered in orange, silk sheets. They smelled like him, spicy and perfumed. I hugged them to my body. It was the only thank you I could say.

"Good." Was all that Grish managed.

"Would you like coffee?" I knew he would refuse, but I had to offer.

"I only drink tea."

"Sorry I still don't have any. But I am going shopping today. For food."

What do you say to someone who is excited about buying food? He didn't know either.

"Wait here." He said again and left. And like the last time I left my door open and went to make my bed.

My bed.

My heart burst from my chest.

"Jane?" Grish called to me.

He just shook his head when my head popped out of the bedroom. "Well, I had to go put it down." I raised an eyebrow and cocked my head.

He walked by me and into my kitchen. In his hand, he held two cups, one teaspoon and a tin container with faded artwork.

"Now you have tea."

He placed the treasure on my kitchen table and sat down. I grinned at him holding back laughter.

"Tell me about your new job Jane." I froze. I didn't want to tell this lovely man about my new job. What if he hated me after? What if he came to the bar? I didn't know which prospect terrified me more.

"I work at a bar."

He nodded. "Is that why you sleep so late?" it was barely quarter to eight.

"Yes."

He nodded to himself some more. "Where are your parents?" he looked up at me as I put a steaming cup of tea in front of him.

"They died."

The pain in his eyes was palatable. "Oh, I'm so sorry…"

"It's OK. It happened when I was very little. A car accident, cliché I know. I went to live with my mom's brother." My body shivered as I thought of him. I cleared my head. "Turns out he wasn't very good with money. He liked gambling. Ha." It wasn't real laughter. It was that crazed maniacal - I have been completely blindsided - kind of a ha. "When he finally died, he had so many debts. His debts had debts, and as his only living relative, I inherited his estate and all his debt."

"Is that how you have come to be here?"

"Well partly." I wasn't quite ready to tell him the whole story.

"When my family first came here from India, we stayed with some family friends. My father was a successful businessman in India and we had some savings. Turns out that his business partner had some shady dealings and my father lost it all. We lived day by day, in shelters and sometimes under bridges for a long time. I was a kid so I don't exactly know how long. My mother tried to make me forget what hunger was by keeping me entertained." His lips curved a little at the memory of his mother. "My father worked hard, and he started a new business. He was successful once again, and we never went without."

I sat down at the table blowing at my hot coffee. Grish opened the cookie packet he brought. He grabbed one and dipped it into his tea. He sucked at the crumbling dough.

"Is that how you came to be here?" I asked him.

He gave me a crooked smile. "Partly."

We shared a small laugh.

"Tell me Jane, are you educated?"

The question took me by surprise. It wasn't offensive or hurtful, just blunt. Later I would learn that that is what Grish was, honest and blunt. Even when it hurt. Even when it wasn't meant to.

"I was half way through a literature degree when he died."

"Literature?"

"*Yes*, I love to read and write."

"Oh, so you write?"

"No, but I'd like to one day."

"When?"

"One day."

"Why not today?"

"I'm tired."

Grish's face scrunched up into something unrecognisable. "We are all tired. Why are you working in a bar?"

"Cause I need to pay rent and eat food and pay debts." I didn't really raise my voice but suddenly I felt guilty for not even yelling.

"OK, we all have responsibilities."

I huffed in agreement and grabbed a cookie stuffing it into my mouth.

"Why not write before work?"

"Because…"

"Because?"

"I have no inspiration that's why. I have tried and tried. Nothing happened the page remains blank; the pencil just sits there and laughs at me."

"I see."

"Do you?"

"You haven't lived yet."

"Excuse me?" I crossed my arms. "I just told you, dead parents, dead uncle, debts…"

"That's not your life. That's their life."

I wanted to argue. But maybe he had a point. All those feeling of mystery and self-inflicted pain, the tears and agony, the loss, they were old. I had dealt with them and left them behind, and although they scared me deeply and irrevocably, I had nothing new. Well. Almost nothing.

"I can see the wheels spinning in your head."

I could feel my brain, as it kicked in to gear, I could feel the seed of a story, the something that could become something bigger.

"Yes." It was a whisper, but it was excited and petrified.

We drank and ate in relative silence after that. Something comfortable settled between us as something dark and big settled inside my head. Words and swirls of ideas came pouring in.

I should have written down whatever that idea was, because when I woke up from a nap I took before work, it was gone. I searched for it. I replayed the conversation with Grish in my head, but the swirls had vanished into white wisps, and as I tried to catch the smoke it vaporized in my empty hands.

When I opened my door to leave for work, I found a 96-page notebook and a black pen at my doorstep.

Jane's stories.

The curly letters were written in calligraphy. I picked up the book and pushed back the tears from my eyes. I didn't want to have to redo my makeup.

I went back inside and put the notebook under my pillow. It was my most treasured possession and I would start using it tomorrow.

2005

My new book was launched a week ago. My fourth in a series of five. The publisher released one every six months. I had one more to go, but I didn't have to think about it, well not for another day or two. For now, my work was done.

The publisher had what it wanted, the ink was dry on all the contracts, and much like its predecessors, book number four shot to the number one slot in a day and a half after its release.

Clarice, my most beautiful and strange agent, invited me for a celebratory lunch. She always celebrated everything. She celebrated the first time a publisher asked to read more, and when a fifth one actually picked it up. When it went to number 10 in the bestselling list and then as it crept to number one. She wanted to celebrate when my contract was bought out by a bigger publishing house and when we signed a future six-book deal.

There were so many celebrations with her. It was amazing and exhausting. Amazing my liver still functioned that is. Her belief in me was almost as bottomless as Grish's, and her appetite for alcohol, much the same.

In the last year, I ditched her a lot. I told her I had to write, and I did. I probably didn't have to write the first two books at once, but they just poured out of me like a torrent, like a delicious endless dream that came true on paper, and everywhere else.

But this time I wasn't getting away, so when she called, I went out. We laughed, a lot which was a given when you mix Clarice with alcohol. We ate and joked and she was already asking about a new series.

I hadn't talked to Gabriel about anything new yet. Would there be anything new? Would there be more of Gabriel? Or would I have to release him? The thought made me uneasy and so I told her I was still planning, she let it go easily enough. She just got a very big payday.

When I arrived back at my building, a car was parked in my parking spot. Well, that's not entirely true. Only half a car was in my parking spot. A stunning, slick, charcoal Maserati parked in its own parking spot, yet it went over the white line which meant the driver I paid to get me home, could not squeeze my Honda into it. I frowned and huffed. I had no time for this shit. It was interfering with my good mood.

I called up to the front desk and explained the problem, requesting they call the tenant down to move his car. A few minutes later they called back explaining he was not picking up his phone.

It took my driver twenty minutes to find a parking spot which charged by the hour. I stormed through the lobby and up to my 37th floor. My foot thumped the carpet on the elevator as I watched the lights take their time pushing up. I burst through the door barely waiting for it to open, and marched to the only other door on the floor. Just two.

I pounded on the door. I don't know how long I pounded for, but after a while when the pain began to set in, I heard a man's voice echo into the apartment.

"I'm coming." It was angry but not urgent.

The door swung open and I swallowed all the words that were about to fly from my mouth.

The man filled the doorway with his broad shoulders and muscular upper body. His body still peppered with water droplets that were casually falling from the tips of his wet black hair.

He looked like a tiger that had just been swimming and interrupted during a hunt. The towel hung around the narrow V of his hips and for a second all I wanted to be was that towel.

"How did you get up here?"

He had a slight accent and his lip curled in a scowl; his icy blue eyes frozen.

"I live here." I could smell the alcohol from my breath and wished I had gotten a mint.

He ran a hand through his dripping hair and brushed his wet hand on the back of his towel. I pried my eyes away from his hand and back to his eyes. "You have the wrong apartment." He growled something in a different language. It sounded both guttural and melodic, then tried to close his door.

I stuck my foot in the way and pushed it open unsuccessfully against his much bigger body. "Hey. Don't you close your door in my face."

"Listen here lady," he opened the door wide again and took a step toward me, closing the distance, so that I had to take a backwards step into the hallway. I could smell his shampoo and soap, he smelled like a place I could get lost in.

"This isn't your apartment, you're obviously drunk and confused, and I was in the middle of something."

I wondered if that something was a someone, then pushed the thought from my head.

"You're in my parking spot." I crossed my arms and stood my ground.

"What?"

"Your car. You parked it across the line and I can't get my car in. Please go and move it."

His mouth curved into a smile. A beautiful delicious smile that I hated. His oh so thick lips that seemed to have been carved out by an artist were mocking me.

"This is why you are howling at my door like an animal?" Yup, definitely a Scandinavian accent.

"Excuse me -" I huffed, but he interrupted me.

"What is the problem? Did you park your car?"

"Yes? But -"

"And is it safe?"

"Yes, but -"

"So why are you here knocking on my door?"

"Because it's my parking spot and now my car is on the street in a paid parking area."

"If you can afford to live here you can afford to pay, no?"

I think I may have actually growled and I saw his eyes twinkle, that bastard. "That's not the point -"

He interrupted me again, "What kind of car is it?"

"It's a Honda…"

Before I could finish my sentence his mouth split into a full grin, he was actually laughing at me. "It will be fine, no one steals those."

With that, he retreated backwards and slammed the door in my face.

I stood there stunned, waiting for the vapour of his after-shave and shampoo to evaporate and for the rage to dissipate slightly so I could think.

I stormed into my apartment. Closed my eyes and took a long breath. When I opened them, I spotted Gabe standing by the window looking down onto the city.

"Lunch was that good then?"

"It wasn't lunch." I snapped at him and he was by my side in seconds.

"What is it?"

"Our neighbour is a dick."

Gabe smiled. He liked it when I hated other men. "What happened?"

I told him. He got that look in his eye. That angry brooding look, his shoulders squared and his back straightened. "Do you want me to take care of him?"

"No," I huffed.

"Do you want me to take care of you?"

"I'm not in any kind of mood." I pushed by him, but he grabbed my wrist pulling me back to him. I pushed against him but he pulled me closer holding my body against his, locking me with his strong hold. He slipped his hand under my shirt and pushed the bra up. His fingers found my nipple. And he pinched ever so softly.

"Gabriel –"

He cut me off with another pinch. He pulled and tugged, swirling it between his soft fingers. Pushing his hips into mine, I could feel him growing. I could feel my need growing.

"Gabe…" his mouth was on mine, thundering, possessing, soothing.

He let me go and I pushed away from him. He stalked towards me, the couch halting my escape. He wound his hands around my waist and spun me around, one hand on the small of my back. Pushing me over the couch. My voice muffled by the soft cushions.

He pulled my underwear off and pushed my knees apart. His hard cock grinding against me, teasing me, soaking me, stroking along, languidly. "Gabriel…" his name was muffled as I tried to lift my head to him. He pushed me down and continued his slow torture. The need for him to fill me growing. My legs began to shake, I reached for his hand but he cupped it between his fingers and held it on my back. I was helpless against his powerful body. And all I wanted was that he take me, sate me, fuck me.

I ground my hips against him, pushing needing wanting.

He stopped moving and backed away. The tingling between my legs a throb, an ache, a need.

He bent over me, his breath at my ear. "You will not move, or you will not cum," he whispered it and bit my shoulder. I moaned, a frustrated desperate thing.

He waited.

I froze.

I anchored my feet into the ground and surrendered myself to him.

He stood behind me, his heat radiating into me. His hand pressing mine into my back. His hold tightening.

A reminder.

He pushed my legs further apart with his feet, and once again began his dance. His cock sliding along, leisurely, deliberately tormenting, delighting, igniting.

I was a melting puddle of need and desire. I could beg. He wanted me to beg. I bit the pillow, sucking in breath.

"Do you want me?" his voice scratched in his throat.

"Yes."

He continued his slow torture.

"Do you need me?"

"Yes, I need you so much." I fought the urge to move, to grate, to pulse.

He stroked me again, my edge so near, so far.

"Do you love me?"

He didn't wait for the answer.

There was none.

Gabriel slipped inside me, his hardness filling me. His body glued to mine as he moved, his hips rocking behind me, thrusting, pushing, breathless, harder, faster.

Our bodies slammed together, skin slapped skin. His hand slipped between my legs, swirling, moving, gliding.

It was my undoing. I unravelled like a piece of string against him, as he pumped faster and faster into me. His hands biting into my skin, his breath hot and heavy on my shoulders. He grunted, like an animal, wild ferocious, dangerous and with two final jerks he stiffened, then his body relaxed, sagging against mine, soaked and slippery. He pulled out of me and left the room leaving me ruined against the couch, possessed, claimed, reminded.

During dinner, Gabriel looked up at me. "You shouldn't let him get away with making you park the car in the street."

"Don't worry, I have no intention of letting him get away with anything." A smile spread across his face like sunlight across a dark sky, beautiful and golden.

I winked at him and set my alarm clock for 5 a.m.

"I can't believe I'm up this early."

"When you write it's not even bedtime yet."

I shrugged, Gabriel was right. Often, I would lose entire nights submerged in my writing, lost in his eyes and body as I knew my readers would be. Any time I wasn't, I knew the material wasn't any good.

I tugged at my jumper trying to suck whatever warmth was available and slipped into my car. The street was empty and dark. The engine's roar seemed to echo and expand across the whole street. The silence was sliced by my acceleration. I pulled away from the curb into the parking structure of my building. The tyres screeched as I rounded corners going deeper into the ground.

I stopped in front of my parking space. The asshole from 37B had all afternoon and evening and in fact all night to move his car. He didn't. Not even a fraction. Well, fuck him.

I parked the car in front of both spaces sealing his exit and switched off my engine.

I knew it would end up with an inevitable call from the lobby and a fine from the body corporate but I just didn't care. Some things were worth paying for. Revenge of assholes was one such thing.

I left the car and made my way to the elevator. I sauntered back into my apartment and returned to bed. The duvet still having an echo of heat. I fell asleep grinning.

It was 6.45 a.m. when I registered the banging on the door. I pried my eyes open and wondered what sort of people were up at that ungodly time of day. Of course, then I remembered. I could feel my mouth stretching in a satisfied grin. I couldn't wait to see those blue eyes.

I shook away the thought. What I should have thought is that I couldn't wait to see those angry blue eyes and scowling face. I clucked my tongue in satisfaction and counted to twenty before I went to the door.

As I opened it, I was confronted with a storm. A force of nature so beautiful, so powerful, completely deadly.

37B stood above me, a menacing tower of beauty. He wore a navy suit that forced his eyes to work harder to be noticed. And so they did. They were piercing and bright, like shimmering pools. His strong jaw was freshly shaved, his spicy aftershave wafting into my apartment uninvited. His jaw was clenched. His nostrils flared as his tirade began.

"You are blocking my car lady." His accent was thick and sticky on his tongue.

"Your car? This is why you are howling at my door like an animal?" I kept my cool, but all I wanted was to pat myself on the back.

"What did you say to me?" he was like a volcano, about to erupt. I could feel the hot anger as it spilt from him.

My body coiled. Suddenly all it wanted was to curl up and hide while watching the show from afar. I anchored my legs and stood my ground. "What is the problem with your car?"

"You know what it is."

"Do I?"

He clenched his jaw. "You are blocking me; I can't go to work," he hissed at me

"So, take a taxi."

"Why would I do that when I have a car?"

"Will a taxi get you to work?"

"Yes, but – "

I cut him off, "Is it safe?"

"Yes -" His hands were balled into fists by his side, the knuckles white. I held my ground.

"So why are you here knocking on my door?"

"Because I need to get to work and I don't want to take a taxi when I can take my car."

"Well seems to me you might be in a bit of a pickle then." I gave him a nod and tried to close the door in his face. Seemed fitting.

A large paw held the door and forced it open against me. He didn't step inside, but his eyes flashed around the entryway and took in my appearance. I tightened my sleeping robe against me realising I hadn't brushed my hair or caked my face with anything. I was au naturel with all the trimmings, bad breath and morning hair.

Shit.

"I think you look fantastic," Gabriel whispered in my ear.

"Thanks."

"Who are you talking to?" 37B's eyes flashed with white smouldering heat.

Shit, did I just talk to Gabriel out loud?

"No one." I shook my head.

"No one?" I could hear the sulk in Gabriel's voice, the hurt, the anger. I would have to deal with him later.

"Listen here, Lady – "

"Jane."

"What?" the interruption irritated him.

"My name is Jane, not lady."

"Whatever. When are you planning to leave for work?"

"I am at work." I folded my arms around my chest and cocked my head. I was going to show him.

"When will you move your car?"

I shrugged. "Later I guess."

"But I need to go to work now." It was a roar, the exploding volcano shuddering the earth, covering all in its path with molten lava and ash; hot, beautiful, deadly.

I held on to the door finding the last of my courage. "Well, if you can afford to live here you can afford a taxi, no?"

Without thinking or waiting for further response I slammed the door in his face.

I leaned against it, my body sagging. Then I pushed off and high fived myself. I knew the phone would ring shortly. The guys at reception would have to call a tow truck, there would be penalties and a fine. But I didn't care. Watching that eruption was worth every cent, and every word written acquiring those cents.

I waited all morning for the phone to ring.

It didn't.

Work was a drainer. It paid well, but it was killing me slowly. It wasn't the hours, or the men who found it hard to keep their hands off my ass and their money in their pockets. It was Leon. The man was making my life a misery.

He would come down almost every night and his eyes wouldn't leave my body, my face, my every move. I could feel the intensity of his eyes even as I cleared glasses from outside. The heat of them bore holes into my back, my front, my everywhere, sending shivers and tingles straight between my legs. I was wading in a pool of my own wetness for months.

I would watch his thick lips move as he talked to everyone but me. His strong hands clutch a bar stool or the lip of the bar. I could see his taut muscles as he shifted on a chair or stalked around the room, following me with those hooded, smoky eyes.

But most of all I could feel his reaction to me. How much he wanted me. Probably as much as I wanted him. I didn't know if we could ever have a relationship, but there was animal lust and desire that would burn cities. I could imagine sitting on his face and melting into him, his skin becoming my own as he thrust his cock into me, his fingers exploring, touching, gliding, his mouth wet, hungry, foul.

He would often visit me at the dishwasher. He would stand and let my ass swipe against his erection. Like he was punishing himself, me. It was all he would allow. I had tried just once to reach for him but he flinched away.

He bent down over me and inhaled, like a predator sniffing its meal. I could hear the purr that emanated from his throat, his hands balled into fists. "I don't want to fire you." It was tender and sweet. "You make me too much money," he added, his cold demeanour back. He straightened and walked away from me. He didn't come back to the dishwasher for a month after that. But his damn eyes were always there, everywhere I looked.

The Hot Bird had a birthday tradition. At the strike of ten, the girls would line up and sing the birthday girl her happy birthday song and present her with a Flaming Finch. A concoction of various alcohols designed to make your heart beat faster and your body want dirty things. When I asked Sammy about it, she said Leon insisted on ensuring every man in the house knew it was the birthday girl's special day. For one, everyone should be the centre of attention for one day a year but more importantly, he wanted all his customers to know, so they would tip better and the birthday girl could go out and buy herself what she deserved.

Today was my birthday. I blushed through the song and downed my drink to wild applause. My throat burned and my body tingled as the cocktail left a sting of peppermint in its wake.

It was the drink that made me bolder, talking back and flirting hard. Leon was right, the tips that night were beyond anything I could have hoped for.

Leon watched me all night, a scowl marred his usually beautiful face. It made me nervous. So, when Sammy told me that my shift was done two hours earlier than usual and that

I had to go up to his office, the birthday cheer fell from me like fresh snow on a burning fire.

I made the long way to his office, it felt like a funeral procession. The end of everything. It was meant to be a great day but instead, I was going to end up being fired. I did frantic math in my head. With the money I saved, I had enough for two months' rent, plus I could always sell the new TV I bought and probably my desk.

I inhaled a long galvanising breath and knocked on his door.

"Come." His voice boomed in the empty corridor.

I opened the door and stepped into his office. "You wanted to see me?"

He had his back to me; the lights were dimmed but I could see his clear reflection in the big black windows. He watched me as he would through a mirror and brought his whiskey tumbler to his mouth tossing the rest of the drink back in a final glug.

"Sit down."

My heart hammered in my chest and my legs quaked as I made my way over to the single chair. Dead woman walking.

Once I was seated, he turned to me. His eyes fell on my face, and I could see the slow exhale. His mouth slightly parted. He smoothed his hair with his fingers, looking for any errant hair out of place. Of course, his fingers found none. His hair was always meticulous, there were never any escapees. This was his nervous twitch. I was fucked.

"Do you like working here?" he stepped a few paces closer.

"Please don't fire me, I need this job," I jumped in like an idiot. I was begging. I was willing to beg. The money was just too good, and the view. It was priceless.

"Fire you?" his eyebrow shot up as he leaned against his table. "Is that why you think I called you up here?"

"Yes?" I wanted to shrink into the chair and hoped it

would swallow me whole. I had jumped the gun and made it worse.

"Why would you think that? I have told you more than once that you make me too much money."

I stilled, my certainty wavering. "My shift ended early, you called me up here…" My voice dropped away as his gaze pinned me to my chair.

"No Jane." He clutched the table as he spoke, "there are so many things I want to do to you, but firing you isn't one of them. Not today anyway." There was promise in his words. A promise that he would fire me one day. One day. When? When his desire outgrew his greed? I pushed the thought out of my head.

"Things like what?"

"Terrible, dark things Jane." His voice was husky and gruff.

I swallowed hard, fighting the urge to throw my underwear at his face. Instead, I relaxed back into the chair and ever so slowly spread my legs, the alcohol making me feel brave. The cords of his neck stretched taut as his eyes travelled up my legs, my short skirt pulled up against my garter and sat almost like a belt above my black G-string.

His knuckles turned white against the table. He was waiting for me. How far was I willing to take it?

"I'm thirsty."

He cleared his throat and unglued his eyes from my underwear. I could see him trying to rip them away with his eyes.

He went back to his drinks table and poured himself a generous amount of whiskey and a glass of water for me.

He handed it to me, the ice jiggling.

I took a long sip then let the liquid pour down my chin. The rivulets of water fell to my chest and down my abdomen soaking my white shirt, drowning his chair. My nipples pinched at the touch of cold water, standing and pushing through my bra.

I could see his whole face twitch. The pulsing of his heart through the veins on his neck. His breathing hitched.

"Oops. Sorry." I sat up and closed my legs putting my glass down. I licked my wet lips and asked myself what I was doing. I didn't have an answer. All I knew was that this was my birthday and he was my boss and this was wrong and right and confusing.

"Don't worry about it." The scratch in his voice was hoarse and pained.

"Damn, my shirt is soaked." I stood up and took a step closer to him. I grabbed the edges and peeled it over my head. My hard nipples aching against the soft material. The black lace tingling my skin. "Why did you call me up here?"

A single finger found my bare skin, tracing a line from my chin to my navel. He bit his tongue and sucked in breath.

"I bought you a birthday present." I could hear the effort it took him to speak.

"For me?" did I squeal? I might have squealed. His face cracked into a smile. It was real and genuine and lasted all of two seconds but I caught it and it was mine and I was the one who put it there.

"Don't move." It was an order.

I stilled as he slipped around his desk and opened his top drawer. He pulled out a small box covered in gold paper, tied with a matching gold lace bow. It was beautiful and meticulously wrapped, just like him.

"Happy birthday, Jane." He looked into my eyes as he said it, heat and desire pouring over me.

I reached for the box and he put his hand over mine. "I think you should open it at home."

"Oh." I felt dismissed. Stupid, humiliated. But I saw the twitch on his face as he must have seen the fall in mine.

"Jane…"

"It's OK, thank you for your generous gift." I grabbed my shirt from the chair and stormed out leaving him leaning against his fucking desk.

I held back tears all the way home. I felt like a complete idiot. There he was just being nice, and I was … what? Throwing myself at him, just so he could tell me to go home? I felt foolish. Horny as hell but stupid.

What a way to celebrate my 26th birthday.

My keys jingled as I pushed them into the foyer door. I wondered if they would ever give us those key cards the body corporate mentioned three months prior. I was fiddling with my keys when the voice came.

"Hey."

I looked down the street to see Barry. The building manager. I huffed, remembering our last meeting. He was wearing jeans that looked like they were moulded to his body, slightly faded and ripped just above the knees. They sat low around his hips and were covered by a light green shirt which said *'I'm with stupid.'*

"Hi," I said as he climbed the stairs two at a time and joined me by the door. His eyes languishing over my body.

"Number 19."

"Jane."

"Sure, Jane. You look *different.*" His voice was slightly high pitched.

"Well, no one left me waiting in the rain tonight." It came out angrier than I meant it to be. I wasn't waiting in the rain, but I was dismissed and wet.

Barry shrugged it off as if he didn't hear me. "Night out?"

"I was at work."

"Where do you work dressed like that?"

"Nowhere you can afford."

"Ouch."

The key finally gave way and I walked into the foyer. I jabbed at the elevator button at least five times.

Barry followed me in casually. "Bad day at work then?"

"Something like that."

"Would you like me to help you relax?"

I looked at his face again, his green eyes shone with mischief and day-old stubble peppered his perfect jaw. His smile was temptation, and inviting him, would be inviting in trouble.

"And how would you help me relax?"

He brushed a hand through his light brown hair and winked. "I'm sure I can think of a way."

The elevator pinged and I backed inside, my back touching the cool metal walls. Barry stepped in just enough for the door to close behind him. In small measured steps he advanced, closing the distance between us, pinning me to the wall. His body felt hot against mine, and all that was left between was air. Air that was drenched in his spicy after-shave and a hint of sweat. The kind of sweat that made a man a man.

Before I could slam myself into him, the short trip ended and he stepped back, his face exploring mine for an answer. I took him by the hand and we crept down the corridor and into my apartment. I put my bag down, Leon's gift forgotten inside.

I took Barry by the hand and led him to my bedroom. I put on the night light I had acquired from the second-hand shop. It illuminated just enough of the room. Barry stayed at the door, he leaned against the frame and watched me.

"Take your clothes off 19."

"Jane."

"Take your clothes off Jane." I swallowed hard my stomach coiled at the demand.

I sat on the edge of my bed and unzipped my knee-high boots. The sound ripping through the silent room. I kicked off one then the other. I stood up, taking the hem of my shirt in my hands and peeled it from my body. I could feel my nipples react, the anticipation growing.

Barry's tongue was licking his bottom lip, his eyes widening with each movement.

I stuck my thumbs into my skirt and pushed it down. It fell in a crumpled mess at my feet and I stepped out.

I reached for my garter.

"Leave it! Bra off."

I turned my back to him and unclasped my bra, I released myself and let it fall to the floor. I kept my back to him. My heart pounded in my chest. What the fuck was I doing?

"Let me see you."

I turned slowly, keeping my arms at my side. He wasn't leaning any more. His eyes pinned me down, his mouth slightly open, his breath hitched, his body squared and ready to pounce.

"Sit down on the bed, Jane." His voice was husky and strained, "legs together."

I sat on the bed keeping my legs closed, I leaned back on my arms, arching my back, showing off. His eyes flickered, as he stepped forward and got on his knees.

His thumbs slid along my thighs and made their way to my G-string. He grabbed it and stripped the small lacy thing from my body. He would have felt the moisture, smelled the desire as it saturated the room.

He discarded it and placed his hands on my knees pushing them apart, spreading me open, exposing me to him.

"Fuck, Jane," He whispered it like a prayer. He traced the inside of my thighs with the fingers of his right hand while his left crept up my body. Barry looked into my face as he reached the apex of my legs, he slid his fingers along my wetness, slow, teasing strokes, then plunged two fingers into me. He groaned with me, "oh so wet, oh so beautiful." His thumb began to swirl around me and he pushed himself up on his knees so that he was in line with my breasts, his mouth found my nipple and he sucked at it, biting nibbling, tugging.

I moaned for him as he elicited pleasure from me. I was close and needy, I began to grind against his fingers. He pulled away from me.

"Tsk tsk Jane. Not so fast." He sucked his fingers and purred. "You are as delicious as you look." He licked his lower lip, "undress me."

I bent forward and grabbed his shirt throwing it across the bed. He stood up, every muscle flexing and bending like a well-oiled machine. I unbuttoned his jeans and pushed them down his legs. I could see his erection straining against his boxers, pushing against the fabric. I pulled on the elastic releasing him. His cock stood firm, it twitched in my hand, the veins standing angry and willing.

He flashed me a knowing smile. "Open your mouth."

I did. He stepped closer. "Wider Jane."

I did. He put the tip of his cock in my mouth. My tongue flickered against it. He exhaled, a vibrating hum rose in his throat as he pushed himself deeper into my mouth. "Suck."

And I did. My tongue flicking along his head then sucking him deep into me, easing him down my throat. He plunged his fingers into my hair as his hips moved with my mouth.

"Stop."

He pulled himself out and I could see the effort of holding back written on his face. He was close, he was suffering just as much as I was. Barry seemed to enjoy the torture of longevity as much as I did.

"Fuck, Jane. What are you doing to me?" He grabbed my nipple and tweaked it. "Turn onto your belly, knees on the bed, ass in the air."

He was commanding, controlling, turning me on in ways I didn't know I could be. Even as I rolled over, he bent and grabbed the condom from his pocket.

"Fuck, Jane. Look at that ass." He took a step closer, his cock landing on the entrance to my ass, his hands stroking my thighs as he hummed once again.

"Have you ever been fucked in the ass Jane?"

"No."

"That's a real shame … you don't know what you're missing."

"You could show me."

"I could. Now spread your knees for me and keep that ass in the air."

I did as I was told. His fingers brushed the inside of my thighs and soon two were inside me once again. He pulled them out and used my wetness to lubricate the opening of my ass. He repeated the motion a number of times, my arousal growing, my anticipation dripping from my body.

"Relax for me Jane." he said, as he gently and purposefully pushed his finger into my ass. "So tight! How is that?"

"Good." Strange, different, arousing.

"It will get better. But this is your first time and we need to make it special." He removed the finger and his body shifted behind me. His face appeared between my legs and his hand was back at my pussy gathering juices. He weaved it back into my ass. I gasped at the sensation.

"Sit on my face Jane."

I spread my legs lowering down to his face, my back arching. His warm tongue played with my slit and his finger pushed deep inside me. The edge which he denied me over and over crept closer until I could not hold on any longer. My climax coming in a screaming explosion of carnal pleasure. I could feel my asshole squeeze against Barry's finger. He did not let me ride out my pleasure. Instead, he pulled it out of me and pushed me up. In a sweeping motion, my ass was back in the air and his cock was inside my wetness, he thrust into me, hard and fast, milking the shudders of my climax until he himself shuddered, jerked, and with a final groan, came.

He rolled off me and onto the bed. I rolled on my back and lay breathless next to him.

"Jesus Jane, where did you come from?" he sucked a nipple as his eyes roamed my naked body.

"I thought you were going to take my ass."

"Oh, Jane, you dirty, filthy girl. I will. I plan on it. I am going to take you everywhere."

"You are making assumptions I will let you."

"No Jane. That's not an assumption. You will let me. Because you want me to fuck that pretty little ass of yours. But I am going to do it right. I'm going to stretch you out, make you ready, make you want it and then I'm going to fuck you like you've never been fucked before."

I wanted to retort in some clever witty way, but truthfully, I was so turned on my brain had turned into a pathetic pile of mush, so I kept my eyes closed and imagined what his cock in my ass might feel like.

I opened them again when the bed shifted. Barry had climbed off and reached for his pants.

"You're leaving?"

"I can't be seen here in the morning Jane. But don't worry," he sat on the edge of the bed and rolled me over. "I'll be back for that ass of yours." His hands lingered over my thigh as if he was considering something then he let his hand drop. He stood up and grabbed his shirt slipping it on in a fluid practised manner.

"Good night Jane." Barry slipped out of the room. A moment later I heard the front door close.

Now, that was a way to spend my 26th birthday.

~

I must have fallen asleep just after Barry left. I was naked, apart from what was left of my garter, and sticky with the smell of sex drenched into the sheets. I showered and brushed my teeth which felt as if they had been laced with glue. I pulled on something comfortable and settled in for a day of doing nothing.

On any other day, a day off would have just been a day off, today it seemed like the universe giving me something I needed. Staying away from Leon for another day after the humiliation of the night before.

The thought of Leon flooded me with guilt. I could tell the attraction was mutual and yet last night I ended up with Barry.

Barry.

He promised to be back. The thought delighted and scared me simultaneously.

I drank my coffee in small sips. Still half asleep, stiff and confused. The night with Barry was incredible, more than I expected from a prick like him, but it was tinted with guilt. Guilt because I knew deep down all I wanted was to be with Leon.

Leon.

The thought pricked something in the back of my mind.

I put the coffee down and scanned the lounge looking to where I had thrown my backpack.

I found it thrown behind the couch. I dug into it and produced the gold wrapped package Leon had given me the night before.

I pulled it out and held it. My heartbeat like a hammer in my chest. It was just a present but suddenly it felt like a ticking time bomb.

I pulled on the ribbon it fell limply across the couch. It smelled like him. Spicy and sweet. Like he kept it close by and he rubbed off on the packet. I liked that idea, the idea that he thought about me each time he held it, played with it.

He thought about me.

The thought made my cheeks tingle with heat.

I reached for the beautiful packaging my breath hitching in my throat as I ripped the delicate paper from the box.

I held it in my hand. The navy-blue box was plush and decadent. Made for something beautiful and delicate. Jewellery?

My fingers brushed the plush material. My breathing accelerated as I pushed it open.

I stared at his gift.

Anger and heat flooded my veins. I threw the box on the couch and reached for my phone. I stared at the white screen for a few seconds before I threw it back down. After a quick glance at the box, I picked it up again. Undecided, I reached for my phone for a second time. I opened up my messages. My fingers twitching over the letters. I didn't know what to say, where to start? How to express my feelings? How the hell did I feel?

I put my phone down once more and reached for the box.

I opened it and reached inside. A white paper stuck up from behind the interior, I didn't see the card the first time and pulled it out. Written in perfect handwriting and hardened edges on marbled white paper:

Because it can't be me touching your skin.
Happy birthday Jane.

He didn't sign his name, but I wished he had. I looked at the words reading them again and again. I put the card down and took the rest of the contents out, and laid them on the couch. A red sheer lace cut-out bra and panties with a sultry floral design. I could feel the pooling between my legs. My imagination sparked with a thousand dirty thoughts, a hundred different needs and desires.

I rushed to my bedroom and stripped, then changed into my gift, imagining Leon's hands anywhere and everywhere the soft material touched. I could see my nipples peek through the red lace of the bra, and the light tuft of hair that hid all that lay beyond the underwear.

I wanted Leon to be there in that room with me.

To see me.

To want me.

To take me - because it can't be me on your skin - what the hell was I meant to do with that information?

I grabbed my phone and dialled.

He answered after the first ring, a breathless hello.

"I opened your gift."

The silence stretched on for so long I wasn't sure if he heard me. I was about to speak again when he asked, "Do you like it?"

"I do like it. A lot."

"I'm glad." His voice was strained.

"Is that what you tell all your employees?"

"No. I've never bought any of my other *employees* birthday presents."

My heart fluttered at his confession. "I'm wearing it right now." I could hear his breath hitch.

"Does it fit?"

"Like it's my own skin." He made a sound that could have been a groan. "Why did you give it to me?"

"Didn't you get the card Jane?"

"I got your card, you can't do this."

"Can't do what Jane?"

"This."

"And what is this exactly? What should I not be doing?" his voice was a low growl.

"Making me feel like this."

"Tell me how I make you feel Jane."

"Hot and horny. I want you on my skin. You." I whispered the last and that agonised sound escaped him again.

"What do you want me to do to you Jane?"

"You know what I want."

"Tell me." He sounded strained. Desperate.

"No. You tell me! Tell me what you would do if you were here right now."

There was a long, frustrated sigh from the other side of the phone.

"I know you want me." He didn't answer. "Why won't you just put us both out of our misery?"

"Jane." It was a low growl, possessive, daring. "I will, I intend on taking you, on making you scream out my name and break in my arms. But not yet, we need each other first."

"I can get another job." My voice shook, the image of Leon caging me in his arms, coaxing pleasure from my body, my mouth, my everything.

"Can you?" I could almost hear the smirk on his mouth. "One that pays as well as I do? One that helps pay your rent and your debts?"

"How do you know about those?" I could feel the heat rise to my cheeks. He remained silent and I wondered what else Scott had told him. Scott.

"Is this only about work? Is there no other reason?"

He remained silent for a moment. "No." He was lying, I could hear it in his voice.

"Well then I quit!"

"If you quit, you'll never see me again and I won't come after you. I'll never touch you or taste you or take you. The only way this works is that you work for me and when time's up I'll fire you."

"Control freak." I covered my mouth as soon as I said it expecting a scolding, instead, I was sure I heard him chuckle. "What if I become the world's shittiest employee?"

"Impossible, considering you're already pretty crap at what you actually do."

"Excuse me?" I could swear that I could hear him smiling on the other side of the phone.

He ignored me. "Will you wear your gift to work tomorrow?"

"Maybe."

"Jane." I could hear his impatience, his eagerness.

"Maybe."

Leon growled, "Jane."

"I have to go."

"Where?"

"It's my day off and I have things to see, people to do."

"Who? Jane? What people?"

"Goodbye Leon."

I hung up, with his voice still calling my name down the other end.

I felt great. Fuck him, he didn't hold all the power. Let him think of me. Let him think of me with another man, with someone else's hands all over me.

My nipples pinched against the lace thinking of his reaction.

I jumped on my bed and my eye caught the curled corner of a notebook. I reached under the bed, Grish's curly writing on the plain and still empty notebook staring at me.

I ran my fingers along the empty crisp pages, the blue lines and endless potential.

I grabbed a pen and stared at the first blank page. It stared back, daring me to write all the thoughts swirling in my head, all the want and desire all the aching to be had, the unanswered needs. So I did.

On the night of my 26th and one day of existence I

conjured Gabriel out of my imagination, he became real in a puff of smoke.

All of Leon's smouldering looks and loaded promises, Barry's demands and sexual domineering and Grish's kindness and gentleness became a single human. A single being that understood and catered to the needs of my heroine.

Me.

I called her Mia. She was a short, understated beauty from a small town. She had a past, the kind that breaks the reader's heart. She experienced heartbreak and loss and she came to the big city to find success. Of course, she failed and ended up working for the cold and callous Gabriel. When we meet him, he is aloof and hardened, perfect in every physical way. Tall, muscular, square jawed, tortured eyes.

The attraction was instantaneous but like any good book, the slow burn and intensity lasted over two hundred pages of games and almosts. Like when she became sick and he took care of her, showing a gentle sensitive side. Like the time she found out he owned a rescue shelter for dogs and spent his weekends caring for them, buying supplies and food. Like the time she caught him just staring at her with a dark tortured expression. And when they got together. Oh god, the sex burned the pages it was written on. Smoke came off my pen as I described body parts; swirling tongues on pinched nipples, soft fingers and hard cocks, wet mouths and tight pussies, slick fingers and earth-shattering orgasms.

I wrote all through the night, my hand cramping while furiously scribbling all over the page. My body aching with my written words, needing to experience the want and surrender of my characters. I wanted Gabriel in the same way that I wanted Leon, in the same ferocity in which I'd had Barry.

My hand dropped the pen and found its way into my underwear. I was so needy, so wet. And suddenly the hand wasn't mine, it was Gabriel's. Daring and demanding. He pushed into me with his fingers eliciting a moan I had been saving for Leon. His other hand travelled to my bra, he teased a nipple with a soft finger rubbing the floral lace, using its softness to torment. He was gentle as his fingers circled around me in slow motion, urging my hips to grind against them, increasing pace, circling, pushing, pounding. I came biting my pillow. Needing so much more.

I took a week off work and continued to write. Sammy was understanding when I asked. In the six months I had been working at The Hot Bird, I had never asked for time off.

On the third day, Leon called.

"Why haven't you been at work?"

"I haven't been feeling well."

"You don't sound sick."

"Why do you care?"

"The customers have been asking about you." His voice was curt and frustrated.

"The customers?" I huffed, I was irritated with his stupid answer. "You can tell your customers, that I'll be back in on Tuesday. Maybe."

"Jane?"

"What?"

"Feel better." The phone went dead.

On the fourth day, my oven stopped working. I was never a great cook or baker but I was great at heating things up. Without a microwave, most of my meals went into the oven for a quick heat. They tasted better anyway.

I found Barry's card buried under a stack of fridge magnets and flipped the card in my hand. It's not that I liked

Barry. I didn't, but I thought after being the first man to stick a finger up my ass he might have called, or sent flowers or maybe showed up again.

He picked up on the fourth ring out of breath. "This is Barry."

"Hi Barry, this is Jane."

"I've been wondering when you'd call me."

I rolled my eyes at the oven "It's not like that. My oven stopped working."

"Oh." Was he disappointed? I actually think he was. A thought occurred to me just then. Barry didn't call women. Women called Barry. He was the one that was kept waiting. Suddenly my day got better.

"When can you get here?"

"Can you smell gas?"

"No."

"I'll be there in about an hour."

"OK."

He hung up. I had one hour. I grabbed my notebook and wrote. Mia and Gabriel were edging ever closer to their happily ever after. I was jealous of them. They had found each other and were perfect for one another and here I was waiting for the wrong man.

He was late. By three hours. He wore a grey singlet that showed off every curved and moulded muscle. And dirty work pants. A heavy tool belt sagged around his hips.

"Number 19." His face split into a smile when he saw me.

"Jane."

"Sure." His eyes did the shameless trip up and down my body. I guessed now that he knew what I looked like naked, clothes didn't really matter. My hair was up in a bun and I wore one of my favourite black singlets, the band name had faded and flaked off long ago, it was too long, flagging around my armpits showing off the black bra I wore beneath. The hem of my black hot-pants showed just beneath. He gave an appreciative nod and walked by me and straight to the kitchen.

I followed him in and he studied my oven. "I thought I might hear from you, Jane."

He didn't turn around. "Why would you have heard from me?"

He turned around and leaned against the oven. "Did you not have fun the other night?"

"I did."

"So?"

"So why didn't you call me?"

He didn't answer. He stood, stoic pinning me with a heated look.

"Are you going to fix my oven?"

"I could."

"But?"

"But it will cost you." He still hadn't moved, but his eyes had grown darker, hungrier, I had seen him turn to this beast before and I swallowed hard. His words were charged.

"How much?" I swallowed hard knowing that what he had in mind had nothing to do with money.

"Step closer."

I did, my body already tuned to his voice, to his demands.

"Take off your pants." It was an order.

I unbuttoned my pants. I unzipped slowly and allowed the pants to fall down my legs as I shimmied slightly. Barry followed the material with his eyes until it landed at the bottom of my feet.

"Now your underwear." The muscles of his neck were taut as his fiery eyes watched my every movement.

When I was free of my underwear he continued. "Both hands on the table and bend over."

I did as he said. I could hear footsteps behind me. He purred as he approached. I stilled, my heart pounding in my chest as he traced soft fingers along my outer thighs and reached for the long singlet. He lifted the fabric, folding it across my back, leaving me exposed. He groaned at the sight. I was already soaked.

He took a step back, I could feel his piercing eyes on me and my body reacted, screaming for his touch.

"Don't move."

He stepped out of the kitchen and I could hear him walking around. He returned a moment later and stood behind me.

"Ass up."

I did as I was told.

He pushed my feet further apart with his own and ever so slowly, stroked my pussy. I bit my lip as the sensation spread electricity across my body. As he continued his leisurely strokes, I could feel my nipples pinch, aching with anticipation. I felt the cold lotion as he spread it across my ass.

"Are you ready?"

I nodded. He pulled his hand away from my clit and inserted a single finger into my ass, I could feel myself clench against him.

"Relax." He whispered as he pulled out then pushed it in again. He pulled in and out of me, teasing stretching. "So fucking tight." He purred then pulled out all the way. His left hand returned to my clit. The building throb needing release. Again, he left me wanting. Without warning this time, he inserted two fingers into my ass. I groaned throwing my head back.

"Yes, Jane. Relax." He pulled them in and out rotating them slowly as he did, stretching me, flooding my senses. He buried them deep inside me. His thumb found its way back to my pussy where his gliding strokes tortured me. I was close, desperate as my hips began grinding against his hand, forcing his fingers deeper into my ass, pressing his fingers against my clit.

"God, you're a sight, I can't wait to take your ass." Barry

bit my shoulder as I moved, faster, quivering under his touch. So close, I could sense the edge, I could feel the build-up of ecstasy my hands clutched at the wooden table, my knees threatened to give way and then he pulled his hands away.

"So eager Jane."

I could hear his zipper as he undid his pants the belt buckle crashing against the floor. "Ass up!"

I did as I was told. I needed him inside me, I needed release. I heard the foil of the condom as he ripped through it and watched as the wrapper fell like a feather to the floor. He stood behind me, his hands clasping my waist. His cock was at my entrance. It felt like we stood like that forever, letting me know he was there, powerful, in charge, claiming. I tried to push against him.

"Tsk tsk Jane. Always too eager." Without another word he plunged into me, his swollen cock filling me up, as he started moving inside me, his hips rolling slowly, lingering. Each thrust deeper, deliberate, driving me insane, his fingers back at my clit, he played me like an old guitar, each string perfect, the desired tune achieved as he took from me groans and moans of pleasure, demanding my body surrender to his own. I did. My orgasm exploded all around him, pleasure tinged every nerve ending, washing over me as I clenched around him, he released my clit and began pumping, increasing his pace, slamming against me as his breaths accelerated. He stilled for a moment and I could feel his release as a groan escaped him, my pulsating pussy milking his cock. His body lay over mine while he caught his breath, my quivering legs barely standing the weight.

When he had recovered slightly, he kissed the back of my neck. "Fuck Jane."

He pulled out and away. I pushed away from my table and fell back into the chair scouring the floor for my clothes. He zipped himself up and picked up my clothes. He separated the underwear from the pants and tucked them into his pocket. "For later." He winked at me and I shuddered.

He tossed the pants in my direction. "What about my oven?"

"What about it?"

"Can you fix it?"

"Yes."

God, he was so cocky, I know he was just inside me but all I wanted to do was strangle him. "Today?"

"No?"

"Why not?"

"I need to go get a new part. I can get it and be back tomorrow. Also, I just want an excuse to see you again."

I swallowed hard, my anger subsiding as desire surfaced in its place.

"But I paid. You got paid."

"Half."

"Excuse me?"

"I'll be by to collect the rest of my payment tomorrow. I suggest you rest, and get that sweet, tight little ass of yours ready."

My whole body stiffened at the promise. He saw my reaction and his face broke into a grin. "Eager little Jane." He bit his lower lip and nodded. "I'll see you on Thursday."

He picked up his tool belt and walked out of my kitchen and out of my apartment leaving me wanting and irritated. Why did I let him waltz in here and do what he wanted with me? I had no will power. I was pathetic. But I was also curious. Needy, hungry.

I showered and dressed and grabbed my notebook, detailing my afternoon, giving Gabriel the words and strength, the domineering and cockiness to take Mia, to possess her, claim her. My body shivered with the echo of Barry's touch, with the whispers of his promise.

Thursday.

It was like a dirty word on my lips. My entire body remained on edge, every nerve ending alight, every synapse in perfect clarity, each waiting, anticipating the knock on the door.

When the day finally arrived, I showered and dressed in a tight body dress that hugged my figure and stopped about three centimetres past my ass. My black G-string was soaked and every minute was agony, my throbbing pussy reminding me of Barry's promise.

He made me wait.

He was an asshole till the end. Or maybe that was just his strategy. The longer I had to wait, the more I'd want him.

I had driven myself near crazy by the time he finally arrived. At four thirty in the afternoon, I had been cooped up indoors all day with one thing on my mind. I was a sensitive, crazed mess. Just how he wanted me to be.

He flashed a bright smile at me when I opened the door and walked right by me and into the kitchen.

I followed him in as he reached my oven and pulled it away from the wall.

"I have been waiting for you all day." I folded my arms across my chest, he had gotten under my skin when all I wanted was for him to be under my clothes.

"I know you're eager darling and I would have been here sooner, but I had a few emergencies." He finally turned to me and his eyes skimmed my body, the right side of his mouth curled with satisfaction. "I'm going to do this first, because I don't plan on doing anything else other than you today."

He bit his lower lip and I shivered under the heat his eyes radiated. He worked quickly and efficiently, within half an hour the oven was working again and the heat in my kitchen had risen by about 100 degrees.

He packed away his tools and went to the bathroom to wash up. When he came out his shirt was gone.

His body was chiselled like a marble statue, each muscle

curved and rippled as he stretched and sprawled across the lounge. And just like that his stony exterior had turned into a burning furnace and I knew I was about to get singed around the edges, burned from the inside out. My underwear gave a dying breath as it evaporated of its own volition.

"Stand up Jane."

My traitorous body stood up even as I wanted to protest.

"Turn around and face the wall." I turned away from him slowly.

I didn't hear him approach. Silent and deadly like the predator he was. I could feel the heat of his body inches from mine. He brushed my arms with his fingers, my skin prickling under his touch as he made his way over my shoulders. He kissed me then, where the neck meets the shoulder, his soft lips hot and tender, his fingers peeling the dress from my shoulders taking with it my bra straps. He pushed the dress down, exposing my breasts to the air.

His hands came around me tracing the line of my ribs until they found my swollen breasts. With nimble fingers Barry trailed his thumb across my nipples, slow teasing movements. Skimming my neck with his lips, while his fingers were pinching, pulling, teasing. Keeping his body just out of reach of mine. I knew that all I had to do was step back, fall into his strong body, but if he had wanted me there, I would have been there. I groaned at the slow torture; my arousal flamed.

His hands trailed the length of my torso and landed on my waist. He flipped me over and pushed me against the wall. His eyes widened as he licked his lips. "Yes." Like a hiss, he peeled the dress from me leaving me only in my G-string.

"I brought you a little present Jane." From his pocket he produced a thin, rectangular box. When he opened it, a silver bullet shaped plug with a purple gem stop shone inside. "To help you stretch before I take you."

I nodded, excited, petrified, wet and needy.

"Come." He took me by the hand and led me to my bedroom. "On all fours, ass in the air." I obeyed, my heart drumming in my chest, my breath accelerated. Barry slipped a finger under my G-string pulling it away while with the other finger he rubbed lotion, then as before he inserted a single finger into my ass, slowly turning it, pushing in and out, then a second finger, in and out.

Teasing.

Stretching.

"Are you ready Jane?"

I must have murmured because I felt the cold vibrator at the entrance of my ass. "Just relax sweet Jane." Ever so gently he pushed the plug in, slowly, letting my muscles stretch and accommodate to the size. I let out a sharp gasp as the plug settled inside me.

"How is that Jane?"

"Good," I might have said, I might have moaned.

"Lay on your back."

I rolled off my knees and onto my back, the plug filling me. Barry towered above me, then fell onto the bed beside me where his warm soft mouth found my nipple. His tongue flicking and swirling around it, teasing, drawing from me primal grunts and desperate moans. When he had finished, he moved over to the other side.

I could feel the sweat peppered across my forehead, the tension building in my body, the need to for release, as his delectable mouth, sucked and bit.

"Barry, please," I begged, as my back arched, pushing my chest into his face, needing more, needing him.

"I love that you are always so eager for me Jane." His breath was warm over my chest as he made his way down to my navel, trailing small kisses down my body. He pushed my legs apart, my ass clenching against the plug, my pussy wet and throbbing. His tongue slid along my clit and he muffled a groan. "Delectable." His practised tongue ravaged my clit, I grabbed his hair, grinding myself against it, the edge on the horizon, so close.

He grabbed my hands and pulled them aside his tongue leaving me, the warmth disappearing, the ache remaining. I groaned, frustrated, desperate, crazed. I needed to cum I needed relief.

"Shhh, I'll give you exactly what you need." He rolled me onto my belly. "Ass up." I obeyed, my swollen pussy exposed, as he glided his hard cock against it simultaneously pulling out the plug.

"Mmmmm, are you ready Jane?"

I would have said yes to anything, and I did. "Yes, I'm ready." The desperation was oozing from my skin.

Barry put his cock to my ass and tenderly pushed the head in. It was a gentle movement, one I didn't know he was capable of. I stretched around him, the plug left me hollow and in need of something to fill the gaping emptiness. Barry slid inside me, pushing himself until I was full. A guttural groan escaped from somewhere deep in his throat. "Fuck." It was like a prayer.

Slowly he began to pump into me, thrusting against me, his hips slapping into my ass, his fingers, practised, meticulous, strumming my pussy, bringing me closer. His thrusts got faster, more urgent as he pumped inside me. The pleasure exploded from me, touching every part of my body. Blackness tinted my vision as I screamed my pleasure, hands seizing the sheets, balling them in my empty fists. Breathless, I could feel my ass clench against his cock, milking his orgasm which came with three final rough thrusts. Barry moaned above me, burying himself deep inside me, clutching my hips, his fingers digging into my skin, savouring the lingering sensations.

When he was done, he pulled out of me and collapsed on my bed. I lay gazing at the ceiling, my body overwhelmed with sensation, unsure whether to weep or laugh. I was stunned, as if I had been tasered, and maybe I was, like a spark of electricity exploded inside of me sending off echoes into the universe.

"Fuck, Jane," was all that Barry managed.

I don't know how long we lay there, catching our breath, calming our bodies, regaining some semblance of normalcy, it could have been minutes or hours. The bed felt like a tub of yoghurt, soft and sweet, and I sunk into it.

When Barry got up, I realised three things.

The first, he had the most perfect ass I had ever seen.

Second, he has fucked me three times now and hadn't kissed me once.

And third and probably most important. I noticed a shadow of a man standing in a corner. Fuzzy around the edges, unclear, but still there. Like a mist or an outline yet to be coloured in. It was just a glimpse before it vanished, but later as I looked back at everything that had happened, I realised that that was the first time I saw Gabriel.

I kept looking for the shadow but it was gone, instead replaced with Barry's naked form. He studied my body as I unashamedly drooled at his.

"You're a sight Jane, all splayed and naked. How is your ass?"

"Tender." I only just realised it as I said it. The euphoria melted away and reality set back in. The aching muscles, my raw pussy, my sensitive ass. They all materialised slowly, like a late morning fog that settles over the road, the one you don't notice coming in until you are surrounded and there is no turning back, just slow forward movements.

Barry nodded satisfaction and smugness stretched across his face in the form of a smile.

"If that wasn't your first time, I'd take you again, right now."

His words lit a small fire in my belly, but my body extinguished the flame in protest. Instead, I stretched on the bed, limbs elongating and extending. I could see Barry react, but it was never meant to be an invitation. I found the edge of the blanket and pulled it over me, exhaustion creeping in.

"Why do you never kiss me?"

"I've kissed you."

"You know what I mean." I looked up at him as he pulled up his jeans. I watched him buttoning his shirt and realised I was disappointed that once again he wasn't staying.

"I don't want to get attached."

"So, you think if you kiss a girl, she will automatically become your girlfriend?" my tone was probably more cynical than it needed to be. Barry's face creased in a frown.

"Something like that." He huffed and pulled his t-shirt over his head covering his perfect abs.

"That's not how it works you know."

"I know." He sat on the edge of the bed and crept closer. He bent over me his eyes boring into mine. "Good night Jane." He planted a small peck on my cheek and stood up leaving the room without a backwards glance. I heard the front door close behind him as the apartment fell silent once more.

When I woke a few hours later the place was dark and cold. Echoes of Barry were all over my body. My hips bruised from his clutch, my ass sore from his pounding, my thighs aching with heaviness. I gathered the sheet around me and found my pen. I recorded our night together through Gabriel's body. Barry's abs became his, his tongue, his mouth, the ruffle of his wild hair, the smug eyes, the beautiful face. Gabriel absorbed it all and punished Mia in a way that scorched the pages.

I wrote like a possessed thing. Breathing life to the pages. To Gabriel.

I was lost in the story, so much so that I didn't see the creeping sun as it bathed my room in early morning light.

I rubbed my eyes dropping the pen, a sense of accomplishment filled me. I was so close to finishing. All I needed was the cliff-hanger crescendo, the part where it all fell apart for my characters, the hook that would keep readers coming back for more and more and more.

It was so much more than just the - will they won't they, - they did. It was heartbreak and tension and revenge and lust and love and agony and pain and every emotion in between tearing and pulling at the heartstrings of my potential readers.

I spent the rest of my week off cooped up in my bedroom writing. Grish came to check on me twice and brought me food. His smile beamed when he saw me covering the pages of the notebook in scruffy writing and ink blots. Had he known the content of those pages; he may not have been as enthusiastic.

I wrote whenever I was awake. I also waited. I waited for a knock on the door, waited for Barry to come and possess me once more. But I knew he wouldn't come. Not unless I called him. Not unless I invited him in, like a vampire. As much as I wanted him, I wanted him to want me more. I let the phone sit silent as I wrote my frustrations into the pages.

Going back to work was always going to be hard. I didn't want to see Leon, yet, that was all I wanted to do. I stood in front of my closet and pulled out the dainty lingerie he had bought for me a week ago. I put it on my bed and studied the delicate floral design, and felt the smoothness of the fabric between my fingers.

Fuck him.

I wasn't going to give him the satisfaction. Instead, I put on a purple number and my tight leather skirt. I wore a striped halter top and covered myself with my leather jacket and headed out to work.

Sammy came out from behind the bar and gave me a hug. "Jane." Her smile could light cities. "You're back, are you feeling better?" she winked at me.

"Much." We giggled and started setting up for the night.

The Hot Bird filled up pretty quickly once night set in. Under darkness, the rich and sometimes famous could sneak in and not be bothered. I caught a short glimpse of Leon. He stared at me from across the room, his face a neutral mask. I mirrored his and gave him nothing. Two can play this game.

"Janey." It was Marco one of the regulars. Marco was rumoured to be a leader of a not so secret, secret organised crime family. He had a thick Italian accent and always wore thick gold necklaces around his neck. His sausage fingers dug into my arms as he grabbed me. "I've missed you."

I tried to wriggle from his grasp but he held on tightly. "I've been unwell."

"I'm sorry to hear that." He pulled me closer to him, as I wavered between - 'the customer is always right,' and 'I will stab you if you don't release me soon.'

"I'm fine now." I gave him a smile and tried for my hand again. His hold was ironclad. I could smell his strong after-shave, it stung my nose, the alcohol too overpowering for the actual smell.

"I'm glad to hear it." His accent stretched the tee out. "But now that you are back, how about you show me your tits?"

Without warning, he grabbed the pitcher of water from his table and poured it all over me. Before I could react, Marco was on the floor. Dave had a knee on his chest, while Lefty wrapped his shoulders around me and pulled me away.

"Are you OK Jane?" His gentle voice sailed through me.

"Yes, I think so. Just… wet." I looked down at my body. I was drenched, my white halter top showing my purple bra beneath, my nipples standing to attention from the frozen water. I have had more than the occasional drink spilt on me, and mostly it was done on purpose, but the pretence and the game were more subtle. This had never happened before.

"Go change, we will take care of it. Sorry it took us so long to get to you."

"It's OK Lefty. Thank you." I gave a smile as he released me and I walked through the bar towards the change room, every pair of eyes looking straight down at my tits.

I shoved the door and walked down the narrow corridor towards the dressing room which was an extension of the corridor itself. A second door with a lock had been built in to allow for privacy. I pushed through the red door; my eyes fell on the stretch of lockers lined up across the wall when the door slammed behind me.

I turned with a start, my body on edge, my heart suddenly in my throat.

"Are you OK?" he looked at me with his deep brown eyes which strained to remain on my face.

"Fuck you gave me a fright," I shouted at Leon. He hadn't moved from the door.

"You didn't answer me."

"It's just water. He is just really drunk, more than usual."

"He will have to apologise for his behaviour."

"It's fine."

Leon's hand moved gracefully, his long fingers turning the small lock on the door. My breathing accelerated and my skin felt flushed with the sudden change. It felt as if someone had turned on the heat, when all that he did was lock us in a room. A small narrow room. Far away from the noise and the rest of the patrons. Was tonight the night that Leon was going to fire me? I had mixed feelings about how I felt about it all.

His blazing eyes scanned my body, landing on the see-through shirt, my purple bra on show, my nipples erect and hard with the cool water.

"You're wet."

Was he talking about my shirt? Because suddenly my skirt felt like it might slip off. "You don't miss a thing, do you?"

"You better change, you have customers waiting." He didn't miss a beat.

"And what are you doing?" I tried to keep my voice from breaking.

"I'm here to make sure you get dried up."

"How do you plan on doing that?"

In two steps he closed the distance between us. He kept walking forcing my body backwards until it had nowhere to go but a cold locker. He towered above me, his broad body caging my own against the cold metal. He stood there, his gaze pinning me, his mouth a hair's breadth away. His eyes blazing embers as he slammed his lips to mine.

The kiss took me by surprise. He kissed me like a starving man, the hunger insatiable. He gathered my hair in his hands and pulled me deeper into the kiss. His soft thick lips against mine as I let myself sink deeper into him, his tongue slipped into my mouth, traces of peppermint and liquor danced on my tongue. He pushed into me with his hips, and I could feel his erection as it pushed against me. He pulled away untangling himself from me. Wordlessly he brushed his fingers on the exposed skin of my torso then pulled gently on the hem of my shirt. I raised my arms allowing him to peel it from my body.

He let the soaked shirt fall to the floor in a wet slap.

"You're not wearing your present." His voice was scratched, his forehead creased, as he slipped a finger under my bra strap. Ever so gently he pulled it off my shoulder and let it fall. He did the same on the other side, his knuckles brushing along my skin, goosebumps erupting from his gentle touch.

He pushed his hips against mine as his mouth sank to the exposed flesh of my shoulder. He trailed small kisses along my skin, his mouth travelling down to my chest as he kissed the swells of my breasts not daring to touch or peek beyond the purple barrier. His hands traced the shape of my arms and fell along the elastic of my skirt. He tugged at the material and slipped it off allowing it to fall in a pool around my boots.

He stepped back. His chest heaving. His beautiful face twisted with torment, an internal battle raging, vulnerability peeking from beyond the usual barrier of self-control.

Fists pumping.

Open closed, open closed, in rhythm.

He was set, primed, ready.

All he needed was a small push.

I knew what he wanted. It's what I wanted. Needed. Desired.

Him.

I wasn't about to lose him again. My hands reached to the back of my bra and I unclasped it, releasing my breasts. I let the purple fabric slip away. Leon drew a frayed breath as his eyes roamed my body greedily.

"Jane." His voice raspy and heavy. "What are you doing to me?"

I saw it in his eyes, the decision. The self-control falling to the floor like my wet clothes.

I pushed away from the lockers and closed the distance between us. He stood frozen along the wall, his knuckles white, his chest heaving, his face heated.

I reached for him and placed a hand against his heart, feeling dwarfed by his powerful muscular frame. He didn't move, his eyes alone wandering along my body, then finding my own.

I needed to feel his skin on mine. I reached for the buttons of his shirt, unbuttoning one after the other. He remained still, his attention unwavering his blazing eyes on mine. I pulled the hem of his shirt away from his pants, his shirt fanning open like wings.

I traced my fingers along the corrugated muscles of his flat abdomen, they rippled under my touch as he sucked in a deep breath. I followed the carved path of muscles to the trail of dark hair that disappeared beyond his pants.

I reached for his belt.

"Jane," he whispered as I unbuckled him.

I reached for his pants.

The doorknob jiggled.

We both turned to look at the door as if the noise was just an illusion. We watched. My hands clasping on to the waistband, itching, bursting. His hands shot to my wrists halting my progress. The doorknob turned once more this time accompanied by a knock on the door.

Leon pushed me away. He grabbed his shirt and buttoned it up in a practised manner.

I tried to reach for him again, but his face turned cold, the resolve set.

"Get dressed." His voice was strained. He cleared his throat while the pounding on the door continued. "Who is it?" he barked.

The pounding stopped immediately. "It's Ruby, I just have to change."

"Hold on." He shot me a look that clearly said hurry the fuck up and do not mention what just happened here.

I grabbed a top not bothering with a bra. And slipped on my purple hot-pants to finish the look. He watched me dress in silence biting his bottom lip, taking long measured breaths.

When I was fully covered, he reached for the door unlocking it. He swung it open and turned back to me. "Marco will apologise next time he sees you."

With that he stormed out of the room, his stride awkward. My body felt as if it had just been scorched by a fire that was put out by a glacier. Pain and steam seeped through every cavity, as embers still glowed beneath the ice.

It was once I was alone again that I saw Gabriel. More solid than the first time. Was he watching us the entire time?

He flashed me a telling smile, satisfied and greedy, excited and needy.

"Did you enjoy the show?" I looked into his hooded eyes.

Ruby stepped into the room. "I didn't see anything." Her voice was sour and she gave me a long resentful look then reached for her locker and got dressed. She left in silence.

Gabriel's smile stretched across his face like a wave, touching his eyes. He looked almost boyish when he winked, then vanished into the air. I smiled back at the empty spot and returned to work.

The rest of the shift felt like a chore. My body ached with need. Leon's touch still warm on my skin, unanswered. I needed to go home.

I burst into my apartment and threw my bag on the couch. My phone rang in my pocket and I pulled it out. Leon's name flashed on my screen.

"Hello?" I couldn't hide the surprise in my voice

"I can't concentrate on work. All I can think about is the locker room." His voice was strained and hoarse. I could imagine the taut muscles of his neck as he looked up to the ceiling in his office.

Fuck. What am I meant to say to that? "Me too." I bit my lip as he sucked in breath on the other side of the line.

"If Ruby hadn't walked in…" His voice dropped away dripping of sweet promises and sour regret. "All I can do is sit here and think about your mouth Jane. Your heat. Wishing I was there with you now."

My stomach coiled. "With me?"

"In you." Fuck. My underwear just exploded.

"The way you make me feel Jane… You've fucking destroyed me."

"Leon…" I whispered his name, my heart galloping in my chest, my body falling against the wall leaning against the cold wall seeking support.

"Jane," he purred my name. "You're lucky I have so much

self-control or, I'd be driving over to your house right now to finish what we started."

"I wish you would."

"You know I won't."

"Leon –"

"Next time I kiss you, and I will kiss you again Jane, I am not going to stop."

"Leon -"

"Good night sweet Jane."

The line went dead.

My body felt like it was on fire. Echoes of Leon's touch danced on my body, spreading heat right down to my core. I swallowed hard and pushed off the wall wishing to subdue the fire welling inside me. It needed an outlet and I knew where the fire needed to go.

I bolted to my bedroom and reached for my notebook which was tucked safely beneath my mattress. Splayed on the bed I wrote out the locker scene into my book, but instead of walking out, Gabriel fucked Mia across those lockers, they boomed and crashed against one another as his hips pounded against hers, as his hand slammed into the cold metal, the room rang with his grunts and her moans.

I lay on the bed letting the pen fall from my fingers. My breath heavy, my body still needy, unanswered desire quelled in my belly, throbbing, aching, seeking.

Gabriel eyed my notebook and rolled over to me. "He'll never do that to you." He whispered in my ear.

"He will, and it will be worth all the waiting."

"And until then? You are so wet Jane, so needy."

"I could call Barry."

"So soon? He was only here two nights ago, don't come off as too desperate." He lay on my bed next to me, head cupped in his hand.

I studied him, he wasn't quite clear back then, still a mix of what would later become perfection. He was still just a newborn in so many ways, confused and blurry around the edges. "What do you suggest?"

"Let me help you."

"And how do you intend on doing that?"

Gabriel remained on his side. His face lit up. I had given him permission. He traced a lazy finger along my back letting it slip over my buttocks. In one fluid motion, he slipped his fingers beyond the fabric of my underwear and brushed a knuckle against my wetness. I could hear the guttural groan in his throat, it was the same one Barry had made that first time. It made every hair in my body stand with anticipation.

Gabriel circled his fingers between my legs, his attention focused solely on my face, my mouth, watching me, as he played and stroked, the sensation growing. I writhed with need, his pace matching my rhythm as he pushed me over the edge. I rode the dizzying explosion of climax and convulsed into a chain of spasms.

When I had settled, he pulled his hand away and put the fingers to his mouth. "You're delicious Janey."

"Maybe next time you should try tasting from the real thing." I sucked on my fingers suggestively.

"Maybe next time I will." He winked at me and got off the bed. I could see his erection pushing against the jeans he was wearing, they fell low around the V of his narrow hips. He stepped out of the room. I didn't see him for another week.

It was a Saturday afternoon. I remember this day very well, not because the afternoon sun drew lazy circles of light on the walls, and not because Gabriel and I had just finished discussing our next series. It wasn't even because we did it naked and feral. But it was the day I met Björn. Officially that is.

I wasn't expecting the interruption. A thin layer of cold milk coated my half drunk coffee as I rolled off the couch, Gabriel's hands trying to pull me back, clutching at my thighs as I strolled off.

"Who is it?"

"Björn," came the voice at the other side of the door.

"Who?"

"37B."

Shit. I trudged to my door and looked through the peephole. He was wearing a white t-shirt with a low V-neck and a pair of dark blue slacks. His black hair was wild and untamed, and his chin sprouted a day-old growth. "What do you want?"

"I have your delivery."

I looked again. A medium-sized box sat just behind him.

"Why the hell do you have my delivery?" Gabriel was at my side studying the peephole, his jaw tightening.

"It's a long story." His accent dipped and rose in sing-song. "Open the door and I'll tell you all about it."

I should have told him to leave the box by the door, or leave. I could have said a thousand other things instead I went with, "Hang on."

I rushed to the couch where Gabriel had peeled my clothes from my body and found them in a messy pile. I grabbed my skirt and bra dressing in a frenzy. I found my shirt draped over the couch and pulled my head through. When I popped out like a turtle out of a shell, Gabriel was standing in front of me with narrow slits for eyes and a tight jaw.

"What are you doing?"

"I'm letting him in." I pushed by him as I searched for my underwear.

"Why?"

"Because he has my box."

"So? Get him to leave it for us. We can grab it when he's gone."

I ran a hand through my hair throwing pillows about, looking and rearranging simultaneously. "I already told him to wait."

"Tell him to go away."

"How about you go away?" I threw my arms up in the air and marched to the door, fuck underwear, not like I need them anyway.

The door swung open. I wanted to smile but Gabriel had gotten under my skin, so when I opened the door my 'hey sexy neighbour' smile turned into an irritated 'what the hell do you want' grimace.

He took a small step back then righted himself. "Nice to see you too."

"I'm sorry, just…" Just what? Had a fight with my imaginary boyfriend over you? "Long day…"

He nodded slightly and I could see his eyes roaming my face, my body, my after sex with Gabriel hair, and underwear-less skirt. I wonder if he could smell the sex. The distinctive musk it leaves behind.

"Come in." I moved out of his way at last and leaned on the door swinging it open.

He picked up the box. Through his shirt, I could make out wide shoulders, rounded with muscle. He stepped into the apartment and his eyes swept the room as if he was looking for something. Or someone.

"Where would you like this?"

"Just put it down by my desk," I pointed and instantly regretted it. On the screen was a picture of a mostly naked man, only a gloved hand hiding his manhood, pubic hair peering from beyond. My notebook lay open on my desk with the words dick and fuck and suck spilling from the pages. And then just as I thought it could not get worse, I found my underwear. It was splayed across my keyboard like a hooker with her legs spread open.

I just about tackled my desk and swatted the underwear off, hitting keys bringing up more pictures. I buried my head in my hands. Don't get me wrong, I have never been embarrassed about what I do or what I write except when it came to Grish obviously. But you must understand how this must have looked to a complete stranger.

With my underwear now safely on the floor by Björn's feet and at least four mostly naked men on my double PC screen, he placed the box on the floor, his eyes sweeping over the open notebook. I slammed it shut as a wide grin spread over his face.

"It's not what you think," I said through a sigh.

His smile stretched and grew bigger until he began to chuckle. Heat rose to my face and my ears tingled.

"How could you possibly know what I think?" he stood facing me, his beautiful face still split in a perfect smile.

What could I have possibly said to that? So many options. I may have opened my mouth a few times in an attempt to make words but nothing came out.

"It's OK Jane, I know who you are."

"How the hell do you know my name?" I went from hot to cold in a matter of milliseconds.

He patted the box. My name and address clearly labelled.

"Right." I thawed.

"I'm Björn Hellström." He extended a hand which I took tentatively, he closed his palm around mine and we shook.

Gabriel growled behind me and I pulled my hand away. "Coffee?"

"Yes please." Björn flashed me some more teeth. I turned to Gabriel giving him a warning grimace then turned to the kitchen.

I could feel their eyes on me as I dropped a capsule into the coffee machine, the gurgling of water spewed into the cup. Gabriel growled and strode over to the counter sitting next to Björn, his eyes daggers.

I rolled my eyes and placed a second cup under the machine, the drilling noise echoing in my oversized apartment.

When I placed the coffee and sugar on the counter, I leaned forward and studied my guest. His glacial blue eyes peered into mine.

"So, Jane." He grabbed the sugar and scooped a heaped teaspoon throwing it into his coffee. "What do you do?" the tinkling of metal against porcelain resonated against the walls as his eyes flickered to my desk and his lips curled up around the edges.

I cleared my throat. "I'm an author."

His eyebrow raised. "Anything I would have heard of?"

"Doubt it. You don't look like my target market."

"That's a big assumption."

"Not really." I slurped the top of my overfilled cup and licked the foam from my top lip. "My market is 96% women."

"Well I'm no math genius, but seems to me, four percent of your market is still plenty."

"I guess." My lip twitched watching Gabriel's face change. Did he just realise a bunch of men have been looking over his body, jealous of how he touched and fucked so many women?

"So, are you going to tell me what you write? Or am I just going to have to wonder about those things on your desk?" His eyes flickered to my underwear and I could feel the heat return to my cheeks.

"I wrote the Guarding Gabriel series."

I swear Björn's eyes grow slightly larger and he almost spat out his coffee, "You? You're J.A. Wynters?"

I cocked my head not hiding my surprise. "In the flesh. You've read my books?"

"Well, no, like you said I'm not your target audience but you can't walk past a bookshop these days without seeing your Gabriel character everywhere."

I could see Gabriel bare his teeth like a wild dog at the mention of his name. The model they had on the cover, although handsome and sharp in all the right angles, muscular and taut in all the right places just didn't compare with Gabriel's perfection. No one ever could. Not really. Not even as he sat like a feral thing sniffing out his competition. My heart warmed at his jealous tantrum. It felt good to be loved.

"He is well loved." My face split into a smile and I could feel Gabriel thaw.

"I might have to pick me up a book and see why." The way he said it made my ass clench. "Get inside your head." His tone suggested it wasn't the only cavity he wanted to fill.

My coffee turned into charring coal in my mouth, as I

pushed it down trying not to choke. I cleared my throat. "What do you do Björn?" I tried to pronounce his name in the same lyrical musical way he had, but instead of a magical melody, it sounded like I was skinning a cat.

He smiled at my effort and pretended I hadn't just butchered the pronunciation of his name. "I'm in stocks."

"Sounds riveting."

"It is."

"Mm mm." I pursed my lips and nodded.

"It might not hold all the satisfying ins and outs of your job, but it's satisfying in its own way." A sly grin crept across his mouth.

"What is so pleasurable about numbers?"

"There is something very pure about taking two numbers. Two completely different, unique numbers and making them a single digit. One perfect number that solves all your problems." His tone turned a shade darker, huskier and my skirt did all it could to hold on to my body. When did we stop talking about his job?

It's strange to think about ice on fire. It is the cold intense blue flame in the centre of red heat that burns so hot, that is the only way to describe Björn's eyes as they bore into me. I needed relief from the searing heat of his stare as I could feel sweat prickle my forehead. My body shivering in the cold heat.

"It seems you also don't do much reading in my target market. I am almost as famous as you, Jane Miller." He said my name like a wicked secret, it made my stomach coil.

"Where would I have read your books? Blogs? Tweets?"

He chuckled at my sarcasm. "I have been featured in over a hundred financial magazines worldwide." His chest swelled as he said it.

"A hundred you say?" I raised an eyebrow. "You must be very famous then." I winked at him and he almost fell back laughing at my sarcasm.

"My readership may not be as big as yours, but it is just as loyal."

"Big and loyal, two great qualities." I smirked at him. His eyes grew wider, and he sucked in a sharp breath.

"So I hear." He recovered quickly and gave me a dark look. If I had had underwear on. It would have exploded.

We both sipped on our coffee, while Gabriel's mood soured around us.

"Tell me where you are from." I ignored Gabriel.

"I am from Gävle. It's a lovely town about two-hour drive from Stockholm." I loved how his voice dipped and rose as he spoke in his melodic accent.

"Sounds exotic."

"It's not. It's just where I grew up."

"So why are you here?"

"I have asked myself that a few times." He half shrugged while his face pulled back with that look you make when you're uncertain. "Something about the land of opportunity."

"And have you found your opportunity?"

His eyes shot to mine, glinting with dark ferocity. "I just might have."

I swallowed hard. His lips stretched across his face in a wicked smile.

He took a long final sip from his coffee and put the empty mug down. "Tak."

"What?"

"It means thank you." He stood up and made his way to the door. "It was nice meeting you, Jane Miller."

"It was nice meeting you too, Björn. Please try to refrain from accepting any more of my packages. I can handle them by myself."

"I bet you can." My mouth fell slightly as he winked at me.

"See you soon, Jane Miller." He walked out of my apartment leaving my cheeks burning and my heart knocking wildly against my rib cage.

"I don't like him." Gabriel's voice coiled around me.

"I do."

"You can't trust him, he's rummaged through your mail."

"He picked up our box. Relax Gabriel, it was a coffee, not a marriage proposal."

He grunted at me and stormed out of the room, leaving me to wonder what being married to Björn Hellström would be like.

When Björn knocked on doors, it sounded like a hammer was slamming against the wood.

"Come in," I yelled from my chair, I was mid-sentence and elbow deep in Mia's mind. I needed to finish. I needed to document her confusion and heartbreak, her torment at having to make a choice she didn't want to but knew she had to.

He came to stand behind me, remaining silent the room filled with the click clacking of my keyboard.

"I just need to finish this."

"Take your time." He gave me a wide grin and walked over to the couch.

For ten minutes I typed furiously, my heart beating with Mia's, breaking with hers, weeping.

I sucked in a deep breath. Poor Mia.

I saved and turned to face Björn who was sitting on the couch watching me intently. It was then I noticed the book in his hand. He caught the flicker of my eyes and his smile broadened.

He flipped through the pages and smacked the book on his thighs. "I read your book."

"And you still came back?" I cocked my head and raised an eyebrow.

"This, is a very interesting read Jane Miller. No wonder

you changed your name. I bet you don't want your mom to know you wrote this."

"My mother is dead."

"Oh shit, I'm sorry."

"I'm not." I shrugged and realised how cold I must have sounded. I softened. "It happened a very long time ago. One day she just … left me. Died."

"I'm very sorry Jane, I didn't mean to –"

"I know, you didn't." I gave him a small smile. "It happened a very long time ago." I slunk into the sofa next to him.

"How old were you?"

"Twelve."

"That must have been hard."

I just nodded.

"What about your dad?"

"She took him with her…"

"Shit Jane." He grabbed my hand squeezing it gently.

"It's OK."

"It's not. Who took care of you?"

Who took care of me? That goddamn piece of shit did.

"My mother's brother. We moved around a lot." I didn't elaborate.

"You must have been so lonely."

Why are we talking about this? My stomach twisted itself in knots and my jaw clenched. Gabriel came to my side, rubbing my shoulders, soothing the pain, scowling at Björn's hand on mine.

"I was, but I had company." I grimaced feeling the flush creep across my cheeks, regretting my big mouth.

"Tell me." Björn's eyes were filled with concern and keen interest. "I won't tell anyone, I swear."

"And if you do?"

"Write about me in one of your books and kill my character off." We chuckled at the prospect.

"Deal." We shook hands and his landed on my thigh.

"I had an imaginary friend. I called her Alison, she came with me everywhere. The thing about an imaginary friend is that they don't stay behind." I winced.

His hand shot to my face, his fingers tracing my cheek. "Don't make excuses for doing what you had to do to survive. You've had a tough time, you were a kid. I think it's sweet."

I bit my lip wondering what he might think if he knew of my current imaginary friend.

"Why don't you ask him?" Gabriel's abrasive voice taunted at my ear. I shook him off, Björn's hand fell from my face.

"It was silly."

"What happened to Alison?"

"She disappeared after Josh and I broke up." I could see the surprise as it registered across his face and disappeared just as quickly. "It was almost four years ago."

Björn remained silent. Was he waiting for more or was I just uncomfortable in the silence which is why I always needed something to fill it with?

"It was a short relationship, lasted less than a year. He was cheating on me with some slut anyway. I caught them with his dick in her mouth. It was over after that and I haven't seen either of them since."

"You don't owe me an explanation into your past, we all have baggage and ex's."

"I can't believe anyone would ever let you go." Fuck did I just say that out loud?

Björn chuckled. "I am quite the catch," he winked. "But for some, I am only a pretty face, no one wants to know what's inside."

"Their loss." He nodded, the air between us suddenly charged.

Björn broke eye contact and cleared his throat. Flipping

through his copy of Guarding Gabriel. "As I was saying, I read your book."

"Yes?" my heart rate accelerated.

"I was hoping you could sign it for me?"

"Sure."

When I went to grab it, he placed the book on the opposite side of him. If I was going to take it, I would have to stretch across his body.

"I was wondering." His voice was low and heavy. "How do you get your scenes so vivid, so... real?"

I turned my body to his, stretching across him, toward the book. I could feel the hardness of his pecs and roundness of his thick strong arms. His hand dropped along my waist.

My face was inches from his. The glacial inferno blazed in blue flames. I was frozen, mesmerised. I brushed his lips with my own. A sliver of a kiss, a taste. "Lots and lots of research," I whispered into his mouth.

His hot breath stalled, then his hands wrapped themselves around me, pulling me close. I could feel his chest against mine, rising and falling, his heartbeat, drumming through me, echoing my desire. His lips found mine. soft and thick, warm and inviting. I sank into his warmth, my hands raking through his silky hair, pulling him deeper, closer. He tasted like exotic places and familiarity, like a dream that made you smile. He smelled like forests and earth, a place where you could plant roots and grow.

I released him, relishing the thought. I pushed away from Bjorn, his taste lingering in my mouth as I reached for the book and left the couch. I dropped the book on my desk. And turned back to see Björn's eyes observing me, stalking me, seeking me.

He cleared his throat. "You're not going to sign my book?" his voice was low and strained, this is not what he wanted to be talking about.

"I will, but I want to think about what I'm going to write."

"Oh? I thought it was a simple to Björn from Jane."

"It could be."

"Or?"

"You need an example?"

"Yes."

"Well…" I took long strides closing the distance between us. I slid in beside him, his hand atomically falling around my shoulders. "How about, 'to Björn, can't wait to show you how I do my research, Jane.'"

He swallowed hard. And then his lips were on mine. Hungry, possessive, insatiable.

When we came up for air he said, "I think I like that dedication."

He didn't give me a chance to reply. Instead, his big body pushed mine onto the couch and there we were. Like horny teenagers, kissing, exploring, giggling. Me, him, us, and his lingering smell, the smell that said that maybe this is where I plant roots.

When he left, my lips felt raw and used, while his were red and tinged around the edges. We may have kissed for hours, I was lost in him. In his thick lips and black hair, strong arms and chiselled jaw. Like an addict, I wanted more, insatiable. He was just too tasty, too delectable, so sweet. I needed more sweet.

"I would like to take you out for dinner." He flicked his tongue over his reddened lips. "Tomorrow?"

"Like a date?" My insides curled; I hadn't been on a date since…

"Yes."

"I would love to." It was time to move on.

"Great, I'll see you tomorrow."

He gave me a quick peck knowing that if he was to kiss me deeper, he would stay longer and maybe the kissing would lead to other things we both knew our bodies wanted. But there he was, a perfect gentleman. My mind shot to Leon again, and my stomach churned. Is that why I was so drawn to him? I shook the thought away.

"See you tomorrow." Björn walked down the hall and to his own apartment. I watched his swagger until he closed his door behind him then leaned against the wall, my heart leaping, thundering with joy, sadness, regret, opportunity.

"It won't end well." Gabriel came to stand in front of me.

"Stop it."

"I just don't want to see you getting hurt again Jane." Gabriel gave me a soft peck on the cheek.

"I know exactly what you want." I pushed him away.

"I can tell you want it too, let me give you release Jane, let me help you." He traced a hand down from my shoulder his thumb finding my nipple, pinching it lightly as he continued.

I grabbed his hand and pushed it away. "I'm fine Gabriel. I'm better than fine."

I could see the anger flash in his eyes, like lightning strike in a dark field. "Is this going to be like last time?"

I gave Gabriel a long lingering look. "I hope not. Now let's go write."

I t took six months for me to finish that first book. Without me really noticing, Gabriel became a constant. He was no longer an idea. No longer a shadow, but a real thing. A presence that lurked and remained and became more real and solid the more I wrote about him, the more I poured myself into him.

I found an editor who tore through the pages. She loved the story. She loved my Gabriel and had offered to set up a meeting with a well-known agent.

To say I was ecstatic would have been an understatement. When I put down the phone, I jumped up and down in my apartment. I may have screamed a little too because the urgent knock on the door pulled me from my ecstasy.

"Jane, are you OK?" it was Grish. Of course it was.

I threw myself into his arms. "My editor loved the story I wrote, she wants to introduce me to an agent."

Despite being stiff at my outwardly show of affection, his arms folded around me for a few seconds. "I am proud of you Jane. I knew you could do it." The smile he gave me was genuine and bright, and I felt like all the suns of the universe were shining down on me. "Come on," he said in his sing-song voice while his head lolled. "Let's go celebrate.

"Now?"

"Yes now, grab a jacket, meet me by the elevator."

I could see the lightness in his step, the joy that oozed from his body. All for me. No one had ever been that happy for me. I could feel my mouth stretch further, the smile stupid and delicious.

We walked down the street to the park, Grish led me to the waiting ice-cream van and asked me to pick a flavour. I felt like a child rewarded for good behaviour.

"Chocolate and vanilla, please."

The man scooped out the ice-cream on a large sugar cone and handed it to me. Grish ordered vanilla with chocolate flakes. I wished I knew about the chocolate flakes. He paid the man, and we walked to a bench that overlooked the small duck pond.

"Whenever my daughter achieved something she was proud of, I would bring her here. I was proud of her anyway, but she needed to be proud of herself too. She always picked the strawberry and vanilla flavour and we would come to sit here, on this bench, and she would tell me all about it." He licked his ice-cream his eyes melancholy. "You would have liked her." He smiled.

We sat in a comfortable silence licking our ice-cream and watching the world drift by.

"Now tell me, what is this book of yours about?" Grish gestured with his hand and put the ice-cream back to his mouth.

I cringed internally. There was no way I could tell Grish what it was really about. "It's a romance."

"Oh?"

"Yeah, you know, the usual, boy meets girl, they fall in love and live happily ever after."

"I'm sure it can't be that simple."

"There may be a few complications along the way." I gave him a wide smile.

"Indeed." He swayed his head in the way that he did.

We finished our ice-cream in silence.

"When is your meeting?" he stood up signalling I do the same.

I followed him. We walked down the path surrounding the park, his long strides casual and relaxed like a man who had no problems.

"I'm not sure. I'll have to hear back from my editor. I mean the agent might not even -"

"Of course, she will," he cut me off. "Believe in things Jane and they become true enough."

I just nodded. If he only knew how right he was.

Clarice Bonner was what one might call 'out there.' Her eccentricity was worn like a second skin. Everything from her thick-rimmed glasses that were far too big for her mousy face. Her hair shaved on one side and rolled into a purple wave on the top of her head, her ugly knee-high boots and yellow socks that disappeared under a brown skirt. The hot pink shirt covered in the fake fur, waist-high jacket, down to her too small handbag that meant she had to carry half her accessories in her hands. It was a tragic mismatch of clothing as if ten different eighties fashion styles met in a bar and somehow fornicated giving them a way to coexist as one freakishly ugly thing.

Yet, she carried it with utter confidence and not a care in the world. I was sipping a glass of water when she walked in, directly over to my table.

"Jane?"

"Miss Bonner?"

"Clarice!" she threw a large black diary, a cell phone, a

notebook and a few other random accessories onto the table and bent down to kiss my cheeks. "How are you darling?"

"I'm great, thank you for –"

"What are you drinking?" She sat down ignoring my thanks.

"Water."

She pouted, and I was unsure how to interpret the look in her eyes. She waved to a waiter and asked for boiling water with a tea bag on the side. She glared at me until I ordered a coffee.

She waited until the waiter left, then grabbed my hands from across the table. "Janey, Jane. Let me be honest with you. When I heard about your manuscript, I thought, here we go, another over the top explicit novel with zero plot." She exhaled, a long dramatic thing, that lasted an entire century. Her hold tightened around my hands as she squeezed, her face changed breaking into an exaggerated smile. "But, oh Jane, then I read your pages, and asked for more. I devoured your book."

Her head rotated as she looked around the room then focused back on me. "Oh my, your character development is second to none, poor old Mia, my heart breaks for her and oh, Gabriel. Gabriel, Gabriel, Gabriel." Her hand was fanning her face. "What a man, what a relationship, your writing is so raw and real, so painful and evocative. Tell me Jane. What are you working on next?"

I was levitating somewhere above the table. Her words lifting me higher than I had ever anticipated, she liked my work, she loved Gabriel. Of course, she did. He was easy to love.

"Next?" I calmed my heart rate just enough to speak.

"Yes, next, when we sell your book, we want to sign at least a three-book deal, we need to know you have so much more coming than just this. Tell me you have more, I need more Gabriel in my life, I think we all do." She gave me a wink, and I shuddered. She was older than what my mother would have been.

Next. "Yes, I am."

"Excuse me?"

"I am working on my next book, as you know Gabriel and Mia run into some trouble at the end of the book –"

"Oh yes, why did you do that to me Jane? Broke my heart! Do they figure it all out in your next one? Wait don't tell me, I want to be surprised."

I clamp my mouth shut and wait as the waiter places our drinks on the table.

"Can we also get two glasses of Champagne?" The waiter nodded at her, and I glanced over to the wall clock. She caught my eye.

"It's after five somewhere, and anyway, we are celebrating dear. You just scored yourself an agent." Her smile spread and her teeth glowed too bright in the fluorescent lighting of the shop.

"I did?" I must have screamed it because all heads suddenly turned and looked at us. I guess Clarice was used to the attention as she didn't bat an eyelid.

"Yes darling, I don't just step out of the office for anyone."

When the Champagne arrived, we clinked our glasses and the ring was a soft melody like a choir of angels, the flavour sweet like nectar of the gods. I felt as if life was finally on my side. Good things would happen from now on.

Clarice stayed for another thirty minutes. We discussed upcoming paperwork with her office and how she planned on selling my book and to who. When she left, she had a dance in her step, I wondered if it was the three glasses of alcohol or the fact, she just signed a hot new client.

Me.

I almost squealed at the thought. I made it home, barely, my face holding in the imminent explosion of glee.

I threw my bag on the couch and jumped up and down

squealing like a little kid. No, she hadn't sold the book to anyone yet, and yes, I still had light years to go in the industry as I would soon learn, but this victory, it was massive, important and one that was the beginning of this shift in my life.

I was happy, delighted, ecstatic, and a little tipsy. I needed to celebrate with someone. I picked up my phone and scrolled through a list of names knowing the one person I wanted around wouldn't touch me.

I texted him anyway.

"You'll have to fire me soon, I just scored an agent, I'm going to be a famous writer and I won't need your fancy job anymore."

Three dots appeared on my screen. I held my breath in anticipation. "Congratulations. I look forward to it."

That was all.

It was something so small, a crumb really, but he told me he was looking forward to firing me, or to my success. Either way, it lit a hotter fire inside. One that needed quenching. One that needed Barry.

"19?"

"You do know my name is Jane, right?"

"What can I do you for?"

I could hear the smirk in his voice. Was it because he could tease me so easily or because he knew he was getting a booty call?

"It's the second one." Gabriel winked at me, gluing his body to mine.

I pushed away from him. "Would you like to come over?"

"Why is something broken?"

I rolled my eyes. "No."

"So, what do you need? Jane?" he dragged out my name, rolling it off his tongue.

"I need you inside me ten minutes ago."

The silence on the other end was unnerving. Maybe he

thought we would play a game, maybe he wanted to make me sweat, maybe he wanted to make me squirm with embarrassment, but I was too horny to give him the satisfaction. I needed to come, soon and someone needed to get me there. It was him or me.

"Or me." Gabriel looked into my eyes.

"Go away." I swatted at him.

"I thought you wanted me to come over?" Barry finally rediscovered his voice and sounded confused.

"I do. Are you?"

"On my way."

The line went dead in my ear. I flung the phone onto the kitchen table and went to freshen up.

"Why did you call him when I could just do that for you?" Gabriel's hot breath was at my ear, the heat of his body against my back, as I felt a hand slide along my ribs and settle on my abdomen.

"Not tonight,"

"Why not?"

"Cause I need something more."

I saw the scowl on his face. The flash of anger behind the eyes. I turned from the mirror and put a hand on his strong chest. "Later, when I write. It will only be you and me."

He wasn't happy about it, not completely but he let it go. It seemed like he was going to say more when we were interrupted by the knocking on the door.

Barry was breathless. Did he run over? I won't lie, the thought sent a shiver of satisfaction through me. The arrogant playboy actually wanted to be here, with me. Actually dropped whatever he was doing and ran. I did a mental fist bump and promised myself a victory dance right after he left.

His chest heaved through a grey t-shirt with a dinosaur print. He was wearing his faded jeans, the ones that looked like they were cut and sewn just for him. His hair was tousled and wild, and his jaw was covered in a few days of growth, making his young face look older, sexier, darker. I swallowed and stepped out of his way.

"19." He flashed some teeth.

"Jane."

"Sure." He sidestepped me and made his way to my couch. He sat down casually, his body sinking into the ugly green pillows whose springs gave way years ago.

I closed the door and walked towards Barry. Gabriel remained in the corner, leaning against the wall.

"Stop."

It wasn't an order. Barry didn't order, his voice commanded, and your body listened. It wanted to listen. It wanted to do everything it was asked, and it wanted to do it well. It wanted to please the voice because the owner would reward you in ways that made your whole body sing.

I stopped in front of him. He sat back on the couch his eyes appraising me slowly. It was easy to please Barry.

I wore my white singlet not bothering with a bra. I knew he could see my nipples staring at him through the thin fabric. It was pulled over a lacy black number and barely covered my ass. I was going to make this easy. Accessible and obvious.

"Take your top off."

I grabbed the hem of my shirt and pulled it above my head. My hands automatically bouncing back to cover my nudity. I was suddenly aware of all the lights being on and they all felt like spotlights, every single one pointed at me.

"Hands to the side."

I let my hands drop as Barry's eyes roamed my body. "Now your underwear." He licked his bottom lip.

I pulled the fabric down letting it slide down my legs. I kicked it away.

"Fuck Jane. You are gorgeous." He stood up having had his fill and walked around me. "I brought you a gift, I think you're going to enjoy this one."

"What is it?" I turned my head toward him.

"Eyes front, don't move again."

There was warning in his voice.

He traced his hands along my back, his fingers caressing the bare skin. "Bend over Jane." His fingers coaxed me forward and down as I reached towards my toes.

He sucked in a deep breath, in appreciation. "Spread your legs, hands on your ankles." I did as I was told.

Two fingers found my wetness, he stroked me from behind purring. "I love that you are always so ready for me Jane."

He stroked my pussy up and down, then inserted the two fingers inside me, teasing coaxing a moan from me. "You like that Jane?"

"Mm mm," I purred in return.

"I'm going to use my gift now. Are you ready?"

"Mm mm."

He pulled his fingers away. Replacing his heat was a cold substance which touched my ass hole. He was lubricating me. I felt the cold hardness of his gift as it sat at the entrance to my hole. Ever so gently, Barry eased it in, while his fingers were back at my clit, his touch feather-light, as he swept his fingers across me. The plug filled me as I stretched around it.

He stepped away, admiring his work. "Jesus Jane, look at how gorgeous you look."

I felt vulnerable with my ass in the air and my head looking at floor or feet, but I trusted Barry and so far, all I was feeling was good.

Without any warning, I felt a vibration begin in my asshole. Barry's fingers back. Sweeping stroking, teasing. The vibrations sending exquisite tingles of pleasure through me. I groaned. Barry pulled his fingers away and the vibrations stopped.

"Do you like that Jane?"

"Mm mm."

The vibrations resumed.

"On your knees. Hands by your sides." I fell to my knees, my ass clenching around the plug, the vibrator humming in my ass flaming my growing need. Barry watched as I moaned against the building sensation.

He unbuttoned his pants, enjoying my torment, he slipped out of his pants and boxers in one motion and came to stand before me. His dick hard and ready. "Open your mouth Jane."

I did. He stepped closer. Placing his dick on my lips. I grabbed him. pulling him into me, as if he was water to quench my thirst. I sucked hard, pulling him deeper, selfish in my own need. My tongue flicking around him, my throat stretching to accommodate him. My ass singing, euphoric shocks of titillation pulsating through me.

"Jane," he growled and pulled my hair, forcing me to slow down. The vibrations stopped. Was he punishing me? I groaned in frustration and pulled him deeper still.

"Stop."

I didn't.

I couldn't.

I needed to be sated somewhere and as he never gave me his mouth, I wanted him to crave that feeling of want.

"Stop," he growled and curled his fist around my hair pulling my head away and up, so our eyes met. "Eager, horny Jane."

He stepped back and allowed himself to fall onto the edge of the couch. He held out his hand for me. I stood on shaky legs, my throbbing pussy desperate for release, my body coiled with need.

I sat slowly onto his cock, accommodating for the plug still in my ass. I was stretched, and full, yearning for release, drenched in heat.

Barry placed his hands on my hip and guided them against him, the movement forcing me to grind against him, the vibrations in my ass, suddenly everywhere, as if the wall inside had melted away. The edge grew ever closer, scorching me. His mouth found my nipple, his hot tongue swept around in circles, and soft lips sucked, hard teeth nibbled and his low moans sent me over the edge, an overwhelming ripple of ecstasy shot through me, as I shuddered and spasmed around him. His thrusts sped up, his hands dug into my flesh as he pulled and tugged grinding against me, sucking and nibbling until with a final jerk his body shuddered. Barry let out a long low groan. His hands gripped my hips pulling me lower onto him, asking me to take him deeper squeeze harder.

He fell to the back of the couch panting, his hair stuck to his head, a singular bead of sweat rolled down his cheek.

I was about to climb off but he held me in place. His eyes tense, dark, uncertain and then he leaned closer. His hand cupped my chin, pulled me in ever so gently. His lips inches from mine. I looked into his eyes, I saw his question, his uncertainty. I answered it for him. I closed the distance, my lips found his, soft and warm. Barry opened up to me, kissing me deeply and tenderly in a way I didn't expect. A lingering, delirious kiss.

He pulled away and looked into my eyes, then looked away shifting beneath me. That was my cue.

I pulled myself off him.

"Bend over the couch so I can take that thing out for you."

Ever so gently, he took the plug out then stood, leaving me curled up on the couch while he went to dispose of the condom.

"Did you enjoy the show?" my eyes flickered to Gabriel.

Gabriel.

Watching. Memorising every move, every thrust of Barry's hips, every flick of his tongue, every touch of lips, every lingering moment of pleasure. Much later when it was just him and me, I would recognise them as he thrust in me.

He pushed off the wall and stalked towards me, then froze as Barry walked back into the room. Gabriel turned away and disappeared down the corridor.

Barry seemed lost, as if suddenly he didn't know how to be around me at all.

"Are you OK?"

"Are you?" he seemed almost concerned.

My euphoric glow may have confused him. "I am amazing. That was just…"

"I know." He smirked at me returning to his usual arrogant self.

"Would you like to stay?"

Barry never stayed.

"I think I would. If that's OK?" he looked as surprised as I was. "I'll be out of here by six before Grish and the rest of them get up." He was explaining himself, uncertain.

"OK."

"OK."

Barry reached out his hand and I placed my palm in his, he laced our fingers and led me to my bedroom.

He stood by the door, uncertain, vulnerable. What was happening to Barry? I knew he didn't get attached, I knew he didn't stay behind. Why was he doing it tonight? Did he want something more? Or was he just tired?

The exhaustion was overtaking me, my mind fogging. I lay on the bed and tapped the empty space beside me. In two strides he was by the bed. Barry climbed in behind me, wrapping himself around me. The heat from his chest scorching me, his heartbeat thudding through me in an uncertain beat.

He lay a soft kiss on my shoulder, tightening his hold.

"Jane?"

"Mm mm?" I purred half asleep as he trailed more kissed along my shoulder.

"Do you think you will ever consider me for more than just a late-night call?"

I was surprised. He might have felt the jolt in my body as his tight arm loosened around me. I grabbed it and pulled it back across my bare skin.

"Like date?"

"Like spend some time with each other with our clothes on, maybe even have a conversation."

"That depends, how much time *will* we be spending with our clothes on?"

I could feel his smile against my shoulder, but he nudged me. "Jane."

"I didn't think it was anything you wanted."

His chest heaved against my back. "I didn't think it was either. Until you."

Was I really Barry's type? Barry didn't have a type, he had girls, loads of them, all lined up. Could I trust him? Would he give up all his many many many late-night calls just for me? and if I dated Barry, what would happen with Leon? I wanted Leon, needed Leon.

Leon.

But Leon was just a dream, despite his many promises there were no guarantees.

"You can't trust him Jane." Gabriel came to sit on the edge of the bed and flicked my hair away from my face.

"I want to," I replied.

Barry squeezed me tighter again. "Good."

Shit did I say that out loud?

"Good night Jane." He lay a final soft peck on my shoulder and I could feel his body relax around me.

My head fogged with thoughts and questions until I fell into a deep sleep, my body no longer able to hang on.

I dreamed vividly of Barry. Wrapping myself around his arms and legs holding on to his strong heavy torso.

When I woke up, I was sweating and sore, my ass tender and my pussy satisfied. True to his promise Barry was gone. I didn't know if I was disappointed or happy, but I had time now to process and think and digest. My head throbbed. My arms and legs hurt as if I had run a marathon. I stumbled into the bathroom and looked at myself in the mirror. I looked like shit. My eyes puffy and tired as if I hadn't slept at all. I was wearing a white singlet that I didn't remember putting on.

A few droplets of blood stained the rim. I studied my face. A small scratch decorated my chin. Barry and I must have gotten rougher than I thought.

I washed my face and got ready for the day.

When I didn't hear back from Barry for an entire week, I got pissed. There he was running to my door, fucking me within an inch of my life, staying over, proposing something more, opening up, being sweet and un-Barry like, and then never even calling.

That was very Barry like.

I wanted to crack. The entire week I felt the undertow of his pull. It was in everything. I growled at customers for no reason, I scowled at Gabriel who only wanted to help, I ignored Leon, and poor Mia suffered the consequences of my wrath. My pages burned with anger and reeked of disappointment.

On the seventh day, I broke.

I broke because I was pissed off at being pissed off all the time, but more so, and if I'm being really honest, I liked the idea that Barry liked me. I wanted it to be true. I wanted to try and maybe find a sweet side to his cockiness, a soft side to his arrogance, a gentle side to the beast that fucked me. Maybe I could set aside my fantasies of Leon and dedicate myself to Barry.

Fuck it. Fuck him.

The phone was picked up after the second ring.

I was expecting the usual 19, instead, I got a gruff hello.

"Hello?"

"Hello," the new voice repeated.

"I am looking for Barry?"

The voice chuckled. "You and a bunch of other disappointed girls."

I didn't miss the implications. Yeah well, fuck him. "Who is this, and where is Barry?"

"My name is Phil, I've taken over for Barry as building manager and maintenance, so if that is the reason you are calling, I apologise. Do you need anything fixed sweetheart?"

"Jane! Where is Barry?"

"No one seems to know."

"What do you mean?"

He sighed, "I mean, he abandoned a job half finished last week, and hasn't been heard from since. His wallet and phone are gone and some clothes." I could almost hear him shrugging, his voice bored, how many women has he repeated this to? "Owner said he must have had a tiff with one of his girls, maybe got one pregnant and decided to bolt."

I stood there. Was I waiting for more?

New man voice cleared its throat on the other end of the line, "So did you need me to fix something sweetheart?"

I ended the call.

Dating Björn was like waking every day from a crushing and exquisite wet dream. The man was just that, a man, everywhere. At work, with his duties in the bedroom. He was magnificent. The only real damper on my moods which were usually chipper, was Gabriel. He had become a skulky mess, like a wolf pacing his enclosure, wanting to protect what's his, but bowing to the alpha. I could see the snarling teeth and ache in his eyes as he watched us in bed. I could feel his desire as he watched Björn move above me, inside me.

I could hear the whispers in my ear, the sweet invitation, the promises that he could do better, make it last longer, and when still I had pushed him away, he became sour and angry. His face drawn and severe.

When we had time alone, Gabriel would thaw, but his spark was gone. The blustery coal of desire was exchanged for an ice blue fiery coal that burned with hate and anger. Gabriel's words became flat. And so did our final book. The book that was meant to bring it all together, tie up loose ends and make our readers weep and cringe and sigh and clutch at their chest as they turned each page. This was the book that would cement us into the history books, the one that meant I could probably not write again for a few years if I didn't want to. It would give me all the comforts and desires my heart could possibly want.

Yet the more I tried to write, the less I succeeded. Sentences lingered unfinished; words hung in the air as I pleaded with him. I needed him to be my Gabriel, but to that, he replied that he didn't feel like he was mine.

Looking back, there was only one other time I had seen him lose his spark, but it was short-lived, and reignited abruptly the day of the accident.

I clacked aimlessly at my keyboard, the lines a slurry mess of mismatched words and poorly chosen adjectives.

I threw my hands up in the air and glared at my wild, tortured wolf. "I need you."

"I don't believe you." He gave me a sour glare baring his fangs.

"Oh, don't be like that. You know I will always love you Gabe babe."

At that, he swung his body to face me. "You know I hate when you call me that."

I smirked. "But at least I have your attention."

He huffed folding his arms across his chest.

"Come here, Gabriel, let me make it up to you. I need you." I used my huskiest voice, the one that got his ears to prick up and the hair to stand on his body.

"No."

I turned back to my computer and began typing. The words might not be amazing but the result would be.

I typed:

Mia stuck out her tongue and licked her top lip, it glistened with moisture. She stared into Gabriel's deep dark eyes and found there, all the hurt and pain he had been carrying, torment and fear. All

she wanted was to soothe him, be the balm that would glue him
back together.

He had not come near her since that night and she needed him,
she needed him to see how hungry she was for him. Her body
burned with want and desire. She craved his touch, the touch he
had denied her for so long.

She knew she had to earn his trust back. Tonight would be the
first step to doing just that.

"Come here Gabriel," she called to him, his eyes roamed her
face, her lips a shining beacon.

Gabriel took a few tentative steps towards the couch where Mia
sat and she grabbed his belt, pulling him closer.

Gabriel was by my side, compelled, he could not resist. I
gripped his belt, pulling him closer still until his buckle was
level with my face.

He was wearing his tan cowboy hat and a singlet that
smelled of earth and hard work, the white cotton singlet
hugging his tanned body which rippled beneath it. I ran my
hand on his abs, flat and hard like corrugated iron. He hissed
at my touch and tried to pull away but I yanked at his belt
keeping him next to me.

Her heart pounded as he lay his eyes on her, dangerous eyes, eyes
that promised all the things he didn't say.

Mia sucked in a deep breath as she pulled at the buckle releasing
the belt, allowing it to fall open. Gabriel stood frozen before her, the
cords of his neck taut, his jaw tight. She undid his button and
unzipped his jeans, allowing her knuckles to glide along the erection
already pushing, tightening, hardening, already ready, willing, hers.

She pulled on his jeans, they fell around his ankles his boots
protruding from above the well-worn fabric.

Gabriel let out a guttural wild sound as I released him

from his boxer shorts. His dick stood hard and twitched as I reached for it.

A low, almost inaudible moan escaped Gabriel as Mia's mouth closed against his rigid cock. Her tongue flicked against his head, her lips closing against him, sucking, licking, as she took him in, slowly, adjusting the vacuum of her mouth, warm and sultry.

"Fuck Jane," he said in his scratchy voice. Gabriel weaved his hands through my hair, his body moving with his driving need.

I was intoxicated by him, absorbed in him, I could smell the sunshine and country and grass on his skin, his muscles screamed from hard laborious days in the fields. And the taste. Like home, like he was always meant to fill me in all the right places.

Mia's nails dug into his hard ass as he thrust into her, surrendering to her in full, as she took all of him. His body shook, his cock engorged, rigid, swollen. Gabriel sucked in breath, panting as his knees barely held him up.

Two thundering taps on the door echoed through the apartment, without waiting for an answer, the handle turned down and the door swung open. I choked for a moment, Gabriel's hardness suddenly suffocating. I pushed Gabriel out of my mouth.

I caught a glimpse of Björn's questioning eyes as I turned back to my computer. Beside me, Gabriel stood, his aching bulge centimetres from my face, his need and despair written on his face. The pain of it. I had felt how close he was.

I heard Björn's steps behind me as I tried to suck in

calming breaths trying to settle my heart. He placed a single, delicate kiss on my shoulder.

"What has got you all warm and fuzzy?" Björn tucked his head on my shoulder and his eyes flickered over the screen. "I see." He trailed a few more kisses along my neck and came to stand beside me.

He didn't wear jeans but had his tailored navy-blue suit on. He stood there, silently. Waiting. His eyes falling to my wet lips. Lips that had just been around Gabriel, lips that left him wanting. I reached for the button of his pants, and just like Gabriel, he was already aroused, hard, needy.

The pants pooled to his ankles, his black socks peeking around his ankles. My eyes trailed his long powerful legs, landing on the erection, pushing through his boxer shorts, begging to be touched.

I released him from his boxers, his dick swollen and hard. Björn didn't move. His nose flared as his chest rose and fell in quick succession. I reached for his hardness and closed my mouth around it, my mouth already wet, already practised. A growl of pleasure emanated from Björn's throat as I sucked him slowly, pulling him deeper into my mouth, my throat. A hand weaved through my hair and he gathered the strands between his fingers already wild already tussled from another's hand. He moaned his pleasure as I drew him in, the hot wetness of my mouth prompting his hips to move in slow measured pulses.

"You fucking bitch." I heard Gabriel's voice by my ear, my head bobbing up and down along Björn's cock.

"Jesus Jane, what are you doing to me?" it was a muffled strained whisper. Björn's body began to quiver. I latched to his tight buttocks, his hands guiding my mouth, his thrusts quickening, his body trembling.

"Jane. I'm going to come." Every word stretched, the air barely reaching his lungs. He tried to pull away from me but I clutched onto his ass and drew him into me.

"You're going to let him cum in your mouth? What about me?" my eyes flickered to Gabriel's pained erection, there was nothing I could do for him, and nothing to say with a dick in my mouth.

I looked to Björn. Our eyes met for a split second and Gabriel's question was answered.

With a twist of his hand, he grabbed my hair forcing my head down, then thrust in earnest, his movements quickening, his ass tightening, his entire body shuddering. With a final convulsion, he found release in my mouth, my name revered on his lips, abandoning himself to pleasure, hot salty cum coated the back of my throat.

His hands released my hair, and he pulled himself out of my mouth. I licked my lips, the taste of him mingling with Gabriel's scent, so close, overpowering, the scent of need, of anger, of jealousy.

Gabriel shot Björn a seething look.

"Jesus Jane." Björn seemed to recover some of his composure. "I wasn't expecting that when I walked in, maybe I should interrupt your work more often."

At that Gabriel growled and I smiled biting my lip.

"Now, how could I possibly repay you?" Björn's voice was dripping with honey. He fell to his knees; his pants still wrapped around his ankles and pulled my ass to the edge of the chair. He pushed my skirt up revealing my soaked underwear beneath.

"Mmmm." It was a pleasurable sigh, and it shot shivers right down to my core.

Björn pushed my knees apart and trailed soft kissed on my inner thigh, skipping over my need and travelling to the other side. He lifted my legs so that each knee was on his shoulders, and pushed aside my underwear.

I gasped as his wet tongue slid along me.

I hadn't seen Gabriel sneak up on me, but before I knew it, his hands were on my breasts, pinching nipples, grabbing them through fabric. I moaned my pleasure, my hips moving against Björn's mouth, my breasts aching for Gabriel's touch.

"Your mouth is free now," Gabriel whispered in my ear as he pinched a nipple, the sensation sending spasms of pleasure to my clit where Björn was devouring me, in greedy, tantalising strokes. Like getting lashed with a whip of pleasure, again and again. Wave after wave of aching anticipation crashed against me.

"Open your mouth Jane," Gabriel ordered me, tugging at the nipple in his hand.

Breathless, I cried in pleasure as the edge came closer.

"Open your mouth Jane. Now." He pulled once again and my body flamed with the need for release. So close.

"Now Jane!" He was desperate, his cock in my face.

"Gabriel," I moaned his name and pushed him away, needing the release, my synapses ready to explode, my body tense ready to peak.

Without warning, Björn's mouth left me. His shoulders stiffened and his face flashed with anger.

"What the fuck did you just say?" his jaw was clenched, his lips shining with moisture.

My pussy throbbed, screamed, whimpered for his touch, for relief.

"Nothing." I panted, trying to force his mouth back to me with my knees. His strong body stoic, unmoving.

"You just called me Gabriel." He almost spat out the name as he wiped away at his mouth, peeling my knees from his shoulders.

"What?" fuck I needed to come. "I did not." The need tearing at me. Hot and throbbing. Is this how I left Gabriel too?

Björn stood up and pushed himself away from me. His face a mask of irritation. I pulled myself back on the chair realising that the moment could not be recovered.

"Björn. –" I pushed away from my chair.

"Don't!" He shot me a look that could melt an iceberg, and I froze in place. He opened and closed his mouth a few times as if trying to work out the words that would not come to him. He ran a hand through his hair and took a galvanising breath. With cold burning eyes he looked at me. "Jane, I like you, like really like you. It's been a long time since I've wanted to spend so much time with someone that isn't on four legs."

He raised a hand as he said it, anticipating the joke that sat on the tip of my tongue. Of course I would go on all fours for him.

"I know you love your Gabriel character. After four books it would be impossible not to understand you have a connection to him. But," he sucked in a deep breath, "He is not real. I am. And you need to decide if you want a relationship with me or him."

"Björn -"

"I'm not finished." He cut me off. "I know you are working on another book, but I think it needs to be your last. Give him his happily ever after, send him away, kill him off, I don't really care. But if you want to be with me, you need to end it with him."

His words sank in slowly. Or maybe I was the one that was sinking.

"Look," he took a few steps towards me and cupped my chin in his hand so that we looked into each other's eyes. "I know you love him. I know it's hard, I know maybe in some ways, he is real to you and it is hard to let go. But you need to choose Jane."

He dropped his hand and looked into my eyes for a long moment. He turned away towards the door. "I'll give you some time to think about it. I have to fly to Japan for a week, I have a conference. You let me know what you want when I get back."

How could I explain all that I was feeling at that moment?

Anger? Sure, but that didn't even begin to cover it. Resentful? Betrayed? Abandoned? Sure, all of those, but so much more, for despite the harshness of his words they stank with truth I didn't want to hear. Gabriel and me had been together for three long years. Yes, he was perfect, but deep down I knew he wasn't real. Björn was, and as pretty damn close to perfect as I had ever experienced. Intelligent, savvy, well groomed, funny, sexy, charming and a generous attentive lover. He had a job and liked to read books, he even read my series, joking about taking tips from my books when we were in bed. And he did. When he plunged a butt plug into my ass for the first time, I could have never told him about Barry and how he inspired Gabriel's sexual desires. When he tied me to the bed head, I could never tell him about Leon. When he quoted sweet kind words, I told him I would introduce him to Grish one day.

Gabriel stood against the wall, his face a mixture of hatred and confusion.

"You're not actually considering what he said, are you?" his voice was low and dangerous, I could see the glint of madness in his eyes.

"I don't know Gabriel."

"You're going to kill me?"

"Of course not. But you could have your happy ending. You and Mia and Spots."

"I don't want Mia."

"Gabriel…"

He closed the distance between us, his hard stomach against my back, heat erupted between us, his hand gliding to the gaping unfinished need left by Björn.

"He doesn't know you like I do." His hand slipped beyond the hem of my skirt. "He can't make you feel like I do." His fingers penetrated my underwear. "He can't make you scream like I can." His fingers found my wetness. He circled them slowly, the lost sensation left by Björn's leaving, rising once more. But somehow it felt different. Tense. Sad. Maybe if I let him do this, it would be the very last time. It felt like a goodbye.

I pushed his hand away and broke away from him.

"Don't think like that Jane. We have forever."

I looked to his face, the perfect chiselled chin, the pillowy lips, the tortured blazing brown eyes that would drown me in pools of decadent chocolate. "I need some space. To think."

"Jane?" my name reeked of sadness and dejection. I could almost feel the crack of his heart as it shook the ground beneath me.

I built a wall, around my heart around my head. I couldn't let him in. I needed space.

"Don't do this Jane."

"Just give me time to think Gabriel." I left him there, shredded by desire, bleeding by pain, seething from anger, needing comfort, love, things I couldn't give him just then.

I closed the door to my room and let the darkness hold me as I wiped away hot tears.

2004

I t took Clarice three weeks, five days and three hours more or less to sell Guarding Gabriel. Not only did she sell the first book, she had negotiated a multi-book deal with the potential for more, pending the reception. To say I was thrilled would have been the understatement of the century. My advance would pay my rent for three months and if sales were average, I could quit my job at The Hot Bird.

The thought gave me chills, it would mean I could have Leon, in whatever capacity he would give himself to me. Maybe we could have more than just a one-night stand. Maybe we could be more. So much more. I pushed the thought away.

I had to wait for sales to start coming in and that meant at least eight months of suffering under Leon's scrutinising, searing eyes. Torture.

Gabriel became a constant. No longer an idea, no longer a shadow, but a real thing, a presence that lurked and remained and became more real and solid the more I wrote about him, the more I poured myself into him.

Barry remained missing.

Without Barry to celebrate with, I started on my second book that night.

It was almost 4 a.m. when I dropped my pen and grabbed my phone.

I opened messenger. "You have eight months to fire me. Tick Tock boss man."

I tossed the phone away unsure what possessed me to text Leon at such an ungodly time of night and not expecting an answer.

My phone thrilled angrily on my bed. My heart somersaulted into my mouth.

"Hello?"

"You seem eager."

"I'm giving you fair warning."

"At 4 a.m.?" I could almost hear his eyebrow arching and his lips falling into a smirk.

"I didn't think you'd be awake."

"It still doesn't change the time." He inhaled deeply. "But I like that you think of me in the middle of the night."

My heart jumped onto the spooky house rollercoaster and was about to plunge into the darkness. Heat rose to my cheeks as I thought of what I could say in response.

"Why are you up so late Jane?"

"I was thinking of you."

"When I planned on keeping you up at night, this is not what I had in mind." He growled it, his voice thick with desire.

I swallowed hard. My stomach tight. "And how were you planning on keeping me up?" I bit my lip, proud and petrified of what I had just asked.

"Guess you'll find out when I fire you in eight months."

"Leon." I started protesting, I wanted more, I wanted him to tell me, to entice me, seduce me, fill my nights with wetter dreams of him.

"Good night sweet Jane. Congratulations."

The line went dead.

～

I spent my 27th birthday working, just like the year before.
My advance showed up in my bank account the month
before and I felt comfortable, complacent even, but I knew I
had to ride the tide. I couldn't just let go of this job because
of an advance. I needed to be paid, to have a constant
income. So I ground my teeth and stuck in my heels and I
was going to survive this place for another six months. To
survive Leon for another six months. Survive his looks and
prowls, his late-night phone calls and growing tension. Two
months disappeared in a flash, the next six would fly.

Like the previous year, he had called me up to his office. I
didn't shiver and shake or worry. I leapt up the stairs my
heart thumping in my chest.

I walked into his dimly lit office. At this time of night, all
the edges looked sharper all the surfaces gleaming against
the dim light as if clinging to the source. Maybe they were
also afraid of the dark.

I heard the ice jiggle in his tumbler as I walked in. His
chair faced the window and he didn't swivel around. I saw
my reflection in his large dark windows. My black-and-
white striped leather skirt rode high on my thighs. My
matching shirt rose above my belly button exposing just
enough skin to show off my flat belly. I finished the look
with my suspenders and knee-high boots. It was a new
outfit. I bought it the previous morning as a birthday present
to myself. And if I was to be really honest, I bought it hoping
that Leon would invite me up to his office.

I approached the chair.

"Don't sit."

He turned around in his chair, his eyes widened and his
mouth parted an inch to allow for his intake of breath. I gave

myself a mental pat on the back. That expression was worth every penny. He pushed away from his chair, his eyes latched onto mine, fiery and strained.

He opened the top drawer of his desk and pulled out a box. It was long and rectangular wrapped in golden, lavish wrapping paper and a lace bow that crisscrossed the length and width of the box.

He rounded the desk. His hungry eyes devouring my body.

"Happy birthday Jane." He pecked me gently on the cheek and handed the box over to me. Clenching his jaw, he stepped away and leaned against his desk. His hands clutched the lip, white knuckles shone in the dim light. "Sammy has called you a cab. Go get your things, your shift is over."

I sagged. I could feel my body deflate like a punctured tyre. I was hoping for so much more.

His knuckles touched my chin coaxing my head up. "Oh Jane, look at me."

I did. His moss green eyes like a deep forest to be lost in. I could run for miles in the hidden paths and never want to find a way out. Crinkled with tortured emotion they pleaded with me.

"Go home, open your present." There was more hanging on his lips, I could see the quiver as he fought words.

The phone rang on his desk and his hand shot up to pick it up. He brought the receiver to his ear his eyes glued onto mine. "Thank you." He huffed into the phone and hung it up. "Your taxi is here."

I stepped back, away. I knew Leon had endless resolve, but that still didn't stop me from being disappointed.

I started towards the door.

"Jane wait," I could feel him next to me, my heart leapt. Maybe...

"I almost forgot." He handed me a smaller box, it was wrapped just as beautifully. "Good night Jane."

"Thank you."

I didn't turn back when I walked to the stairs even though I felt his eyes on my back. Following my every move. I stepped inside clutching onto my two boxes, my heart galloping in my chest. Disappointment turning to excitement. What did Leon buy me? I bit my lip knowing it would be hard not to tear the wrapping away in the taxi. I deposited them in my bag, their weight noticeable, a reminder.

I swear I had the slowest taxi in the world that night. It felt like we circumnavigated the entire planet before arriving home. I hopped out and ran to the stairwell, there was no way I was going to wait for the elevator. Not tonight.

I took the stairs two at a time and made a mental note to never walk up them again. The stink of stale urine and rot hung in the air. Barry seriously had to stop fucking everything that moves and start doing his job. I thought about reminding him about that next time I saw him. If I ever saw him again, that asshole.

Since his disappearance, a part of me always wondered if it was my fault. Did he leave because the thought of being with me scared him that much? Did he change his mind? Or did he really get another girl pregnant? I winced and pushed Barry out of my head.

I burst through my door and slammed it shut before running to the couch and digging into my bag. The beautifully wrapped packages looked out of place in this surrounding. Grotty old furniture and disintegrating curtains. I fingered the big box, tracing its edges, seeking out the lace bow. I pulled on the lace and it untangled itself, falling limply to the floor.

"What's that?" Gabriel walked into the room, his jeans hung low around his narrow hips and his chiselled upper body flexed as he moved.

"A birthday present from Leon."

A cloud drifted across Gabriel's face. He remained silent.

I fought every urge in my body wanting to tear the wrapping to shreds, instead, finding the tape and peeling it gently, savouring my growing anticipation, the tingling of the fingers, the beating of my heart, my bated breath.

The gold wrapping fell away to reveal a rectangular black box. Just like the wrapping, it was elegant and perfect.

I opened the box letting the lid fall to the ground. My mouth fell open as I eyed my gift. I searched for the card. As before it was hidden behind the velvet interior of the box and was written in Leon's handwriting on the same marbled white paper.

> *Until I can fill you up with the real thing.*
> *Happy birthday Jane.*

I swallowed hard. How can he make me this wet without even being in the room? I fell backwards into the couch whimpering. I had wanted him for so long and now he had given me a piece of himself.

"What the fuck is that?" Gabriel came to sit by me and eyed my gift.

"It's a dick Gabriel."

He gave me one of his 'no shit' looks, and balled hands on his knees.

I found the smaller box and unwrapped it, this time I tore at the paper not caring about the delicate exterior.

Two batteries fell from the box. I could almost see Leon smirking in his office.

Leon.

Was he thinking of me? Did he want me to call him? To thank him? Did he want to listen to me while I used his gift?

Of course, I was going to use it, there was never a question, although the first time I was going to be with Leon, I had hoped it would be all of him.

I loaded the batteries into my new dildo and switched it on. The hushed humming filled the room.

I ran the tip of my fingers along Gabriel's thigh. "Would you like to come and help me test it out?"

"No," it was a cold and deafening rejection. "I won't fuck you with someone else's dick."

"It's just a mould."

"I said no."

"Suit yourself." I shrugged and attempted to get up.

Gabriel held me down, his nostrils flaring, his face twisted in an ugly scowl.

"Let me go Gabriel. Now!"

Gabriel wrenched my face to his and his mouth latched on to mine. His tongue sliding beyond my teeth, invading, sweeping, colliding. His fingers slid over my breasts, following the curve and shape of them, his thumb finding my hardening nipple, teasing it through tight cotton.

His other hand pried my legs open, a single finger slid beyond my underwear and across my wetness. Gabriel sucked in a breath and bit my lower lip. I knew what he was asking. Was I this wet for him or for Leon? I could never answer that question, not when Leon has always been part of Gabriel's make up.

He took the dick from my hand and pushed it to my lips. I opened for him as he guided it into my mouth. I could feel the textured silicone, the dips and lines of veins and skin. I closed my eyes, imagining Leon, the low grunts, the taut cords of his neck.

Gabriel's fingers brushed over my underwear, the moisture already soaking the red lace I had worn for Leon. Gabriel's pace increased, deliberately teasing, timing his feathered touch to inflict desire and need, but provide no release.

He pulled away from my mouth. He pried my legs further apart, resting the dildo at my opening, allowing the vibrations to roll over me. He teased a nipple. I arched my back, pushing myself against Leon. Gabriel, pulled him away, not allowing me a reprieve. Savouring my torment.

"Please," I begged through ragged breaths.

Gabriel ignored my pleas, dragging his hand across my chest. Worshipping my nipples with his tongue, his teeth, swirling, sweeping, biting. The vibrations searing my senses, as I clung to pleasure.

"Please."

"Please who? Who are you fucking Jane?"

I didn't want to answer the question, not when his mouth was clamped around my nipple, his tongue forcing a gasp from my mouth, my back arching towards him, so that he could have more of me, all of me.

"Please Gabriel." It was Gabriel, that was teasing and pleasuring, but as he eased my new birthday gift into my pussy, I knew I was thinking of another.

The dildo slipped into me and I bucked my hips wanting Gabriel to go deeper, the humming on my throbbing clit intoxicating, delicious.

He pulled out again, his movements measured, slow, agonising bliss.

He entered me again. Overloading my senses, his hungry mouth still at my breasts, the grip on my body tight.

I was his prisoner. Chained by need and lust. Tortured by desire.

Gabriel and Leon melted into one as he buried the moulded dick inside me again and again, thrusting in measured, fixed movements that elicited too much pleasure. Too much.

"Gabriel," I begged.

He plunged the dildo into me and allowed the vibrations to push me over the edge while he ravaged my nipples. In a burst of ecstasy, my body arched and clenched, I screamed my release, a sob at my throat. I rode the waves of pleasure, until my body calmed.

Gabriel released me and ever so gently pulled the dildo out. He switched it off, the hum dying away. Only the sound of my heavy breathing filled the room.

"Did you like that Jane?" his voice was sweet, but I could hear the undercurrent of malice just beneath. "Is this what you want? For me to fuck you while you think of everyone else?"

"Gabriel," I tried to reach for him but he flinched away.

"This is the last time I will let this dick come between us."

I pushed myself off the couch, the pleasure that drowned me moments ago falling away like melting snow. "Gabriel, you are forgetting who you are. I love you, but I will see and fuck whoever I like, and you will do as you're told."

He gave me a scathing look then dropped his head.

"You're right Jane. I'm sorry. I just hate sharing you."

"I know Gabe, but you have to remember, you're not really here."

I called in sick. I didn't know how to face Leon. He would have questions, questions I didn't want to answer, not to his face anyway.

My phone rang five minutes after I called Sammy.

"You're unwell again?" his voice was a combination of irritated and worried.

"No Leon, I'm fine."

"So why did you call in sick?"

"I'm avoiding you."

After a short silence, he asked, "Why?"

"I think you know." My mouth felt dry.

"Did you like your gift?"

"I did."

"Did it fit?" his voice was a low rumbling thunder.

I bit my lip, heat rising to my cheek. "It was a little tight."

I heard the sharp intake of breath on the other side of the line.

"Jane –"

I cut him off, "See you on Tuesday Leon, I need the day to test out all the holes my birthday gift can fill."

I hung up, a triumphant smile on my lips. Fuck him. Two can play this game.

It's hard to describe the moment that you see more than a single zero in your bank account. I was broke before I started work at The Hot Bird, and although I was earning great money, there were old debts and necessities.

I needed new clothes for work, a desk, some new bed sheets, you get the idea.

I was spending nearly as quickly as I was earning. I saved what I could by foregoing meals to ensure I had a safety net for later.

So, to wake up and see four zeros behind a single number in *my* bank account almost sent me into cardiac arrest. The thing was, this wasn't my advance. I got that two months before, this was my first pay cheque. My series hit the shelves two months prior and flew to number one in its first six weeks. It was still at number one, and Clarice assured me it would be likely to remain there for a while yet. She also reminded me that nothing sells your first book like the second one. I assured her that I was nearly done with the second book. She asked me to send her everything I had.

After doing a victory dance around my apartment I grabbed my phone.

"I don't need your job anymore. I can make my own way."

The message was seen. The small tick beneath the message glared at me. He didn't reply. Not after an hour or after two.

I paced my apartment like a caged animal. What was that asshole doing? He should have called, texted, sent a bloody singing telegram. His silence was gnawing at me.

I got dressed for work. I had half a mind to call in sick again, but I owed Sammy, leaving her in the lurch because her boss was a total asshole just wasn't fair.

I applied my makeup ensuring to put on an extra coat of Fire Breather lipstick. I smacked my lips together and headed for the door.

When I got to work Sammy gave me a lingering look, that smile of hers stretched across her face and she walked right over and threw her arms around me in a warm embrace. It was affectionate and beautiful like a sister would. I held her for a moment and she released me.

"Leon wants to see you upstairs." She flashed me her pearly whites and turned to the bar.

Later it would dawn on me that this was her goodbye.

His office was brightly lit. He was leaning against his desk, staring at the door. His hair, as always, immaculately brushed to the side. He wore a black tailored suit that was designed to show off all his best features. He stiffened as he saw me enter his office, and clasped his hands in front of him.

"Jane." Leon straightened up and pointed to the seat in front of his desk. "Please sit."

I did as I was told.

Leon rounded his desk and fell into his seat. He stared at me for a long moment and picked up a pristine white envelope that was placed neatly before him.

"Jane Miller. You have worked here for approximately two years. In that time your work ethic has proven to be below par, taking unscheduled time off, slow at your evening tasks and your appeal with customers has worn off."

"Hey!" I cut him off, but he raised a hand silently.

I crossed my arms in protest and stared at him.

He cleared his throat. "As I was saying, due to your performance I must inform you that your job here has become redundant effective immediately. Here is your severance pay, you will find it more than generous."

He held out the envelope. I stood up attempting to snatch it from him. Instead, he grabbed my wrist and held it pulling me over his desk. Stretching me so that I was almost completely bent over.

"Fuck Jane, I have wanted you bent over that desk for so long." I swallowed hard at his words as he released me and handed me the envelope. I pulled myself up and adjusted my skirt. I opened the envelope and eyed my severance.

"You don't have to do this."

"I know, but I want to. Just like I want to do this." Leon shot from his chair and was by my side in a matter of a few strides pushing me against the lip of his desk, his firm body like a wall against mine. Leon grabbed my chin wrenching my head towards his. His lips captured my mouth with hungry urgency. His soft lips devouring me in a long drugging kiss. When he released me, his broad chest was heaving, mimicking my own.

"Jane," he whispered my name like a prayer. He stepped back and held out his hand to me peeling me off his desk. I didn't want to move. I wanted him to throw me onto that slab of wood and fuck me, take me, make me scream out his name.

"Would you join me for dinner Jane?" his self-control back, his face revealing nothing.

"Yes." As long as he was on the menu.

The car ride was charged, any wayward spark would have set fire to the back seat, an inescapable inferno.

We sat in silence, his fingers stroked my thighs in deliberate long strokes that started just above my knees and ended beyond my skirt, close enough to feel the heat between my legs.

We stopped somewhere in the city. The street was vibrant. Street lights tried to out-sparkle neon signs. The streets were flooded with people, colourful, odd, beautiful. Leon pulled me from the car and guided me towards a restaurant.

The space was beautiful, elegant and stylish. I felt completely under dressed. My body froze. Leon paying no heed to my discomfort followed the waiter egging me on with a hand at the small of my back. Forcing me to put one foot in front of the other.

"People are watching me."

"What else is new Jane?"

"This isn't work."

"It's exactly the same. All the men in the room suddenly realised they want to fuck you and all the women wish they were you. The only difference is that they will not be throwing money at you tonight, and the only man that will get to touch you is me." His face remained stoic while my stomach coiled and twisted, trying to hang on to my heart that was suddenly racing.

The waiter led us along a long teppanyaki table. Hot plates and food lined the counter. Men in white chef's uniform and tall white hats performed for the spectators. Clanging metal and laughter echoed through the space.

The waiter indicated that our seats were at the end of the long table. Leon pulled out my chair and waited for me to sit before removing his jacket. He hung it on his chair and sat beside me.

The waiter asked for our drinks order, Leon ordered a beer for himself and a gin and tonic for me.

"You make assumptions."

"I pay attention," he retorted. I couldn't argue. It's all I ever drank at work.

A tall skinny man dressed in white arrived at the hot plate. He introduced himself at Arihiro and told us he would be our chef for the night. He cracked a few jokes and poured oil on the sizzling plate, his metal scrapers clanging like thunder. Arihiro threw a series of vegetables on the hot plate, his practised hands moving in fluid perfect motions, like a practised dancer. Meat and rice were coated by sweet sauces and soon our meal was served in bowls, steaming and mouth-watering.

Spending time with Leon seemed effortless when he was out of his office. His sleeves were rolled half way up his muscular forearms, and his tattoos peeked beyond the fabric.

We laughed a lot.

He laughed.

It was warm and sweet, low and raucous and completely irresistible. There is something very sexy about a man letting down his guard and just being himself. His serious façade melted away as laughter lines creased his eyes. He seemed younger when he smiled. And that night he smiled a lot.

We talked, and cheered and clapped our chef. Leon fed me sushi and tempura vegetables. We drank.

I drank.

Not enough to lose my senses, but enough to let some of my guard fall away. Enough so I could be free to be me. Enough so that I would stop being afraid of all the feelings and desires I had for this man.

Throughout dinner, his hands were always on me. My thigh, my shoulders, my chin. His warm fingers never left me, like a constant reminder that he was near. Not that I needed it. My body reacted to him on its own. Like somewhere I had a switch and Leon knew just how to flick it and leave it on, burning, lighting up, heating up until all that was left is molten hot heat with nowhere to go.

Dinner ended too quickly. I didn't want it to end. It's not that I didn't want to see what happened next, but I liked the moment we were in, the happy bubble of beginnings. The hope that lay there under the surface. After we both got what we wanted, there might be more. So much more.

He held my hand while he paid and guided us outside.

We walked in silence for a while, making our way through the crowds, music and sizzle escaped restaurants as patrons walked in and out. The night air was heavy with the smell of garlic and petrol.

I'm not sure how we got to the hotel. But there we stood. The tower loomed above us, pristine and inviting for all the right reasons, for all the wrong ones too.

Leon brought my hand up to his mouth and lay a gentle warm kiss on it.

"I don't want tonight to end here," he said. The sweetness drained from his voice allowing for vulnerability to filter in.

I shifted away from his warm body and craned my head to look at his face. "What do you want Leon?"

"More."

My pulse hammered through my veins as I searched his face. "What would more entail?"

"More of this." He leaned into me, his lips finding mine, pulling me in, indulgent and greedy. He pulled away leaving me breathless. "More of you Jane. Late-night texts and dinner dates. I want to laugh with you Jane. It's been a long time since I've had such a good night."

I could feel the heat as it warmed me. "I think I would like that."

He weaved his strong hands around me and pulled me against him, his lips finding mine once more. Hungry, insistent, predatory. I could feel him hardening against me. Leon was going to give me more.

So much more.

He sank his head to my ears. "I want you to come upstairs with me," his voice was deep and husky. "I want to see you naked. I want to touch you in all the ways I have denied myself. I want to keep you up all night calling my name."

I could feel the heat as it spread along my body, burying itself in my core. My heart fluttered in my chest like a butterfly about to be pinned.

I nodded. I was paralysed, but not with fear, by desire and lust and need so great I thought I would melt right into the pavement like an ice cube on a hot day. I swallowed searching for my voice. "Take me upstairs Leon."

The grip on my hand tightened, and he pulled me into the bright lobby. White and gold tapestries and a high ceiling in an exquisite setting that I had no time nor inclination to admire. Leon ploughed through the reception area and led us straight to the elevator.

I guess he was prepared.

When the elevator arrived, I could feel the tension in his body, like he was resisting heaving me into the lift and fucking me against the golden walls. His perfect hair stood to the side, as if it too was on edge, his jaw set his eyes locked on the numbers that flashed painfully slow as we travelled higher.

His iron grip pulled my wrist as soon as the elevator doors opened and we spilt into the hall. He produced a key card from his jacket pocket and led us to our room. He released his grip as soon as I walked inside as if certain now, I would no longer be able to get away from him.

The hotel room was not like any other I had been in. It resembled an expensive penthouse apartment. Doorways led to rooms and bathrooms, but much like the lobby, I had little time to admire my surroundings where all my focus shifted to the one dangerous thing in the room. The beacon that summoned all my attention.

Leon removed his jacket and threw it on the couch. His eyes locked onto mine, searing me with their intensity. I bit my lip and took a step back as he stepped towards me. Circling around me, he stalked me like a predator circling his prey, closing the distance between us.

I stepped to the right, and he mimicked my move. I turned left, and he reached out an arm, clasping my wrist. I let out a little yelp as Leon spun me and slammed my body into his.

Tightening his grip, he forced my back to sink against his hard body, like a wall that's been standing in the sun all day. Hard and hot.

I could feel him, all of him, every rippling muscle and heaving breath, every dip and bulge and bump. His strong arms caged me, his mouth at my ear.

"I have been waiting so long for you Jane." He breathed and lay a soft kiss on my shoulder sending my heart into a frenzy. He trailed kisses along my neck, his hand sliding across my abdomen.

His hands travelled to the hem of my shirt, he tugged at the material, forcing my hands above my head. He threw it to the ground and unclipped my bra letting it fall to the floor. His hands found my exposed flesh cupping my breasts, swirling his thumbs against my nipples. He bit my shoulder. "Fuck Jane." The words slurred against my skin.

I wanted to melt, my bones turned to jelly beneath his touch, but his strong hands held me up, his body moulding to mine.

"You are so beautiful Jane." He nipped my neck, his hips grinding into me. I could feel how hard he was, how needy. "Look." He spun us around, a body length mirror greeted me.

Leon freed a hand and pulled at my skirt. It slipped to the floor pooling by my legs. He kicked it away and placed his feet on the inside of mine pulling me apart, forcing me against him. He anchored his attention on my face as his hand plunged into my underwear. I gasped at the soft touch of his fingers as they brushed my wetness.

A low growl emanated from somewhere deep inside Leon. His eyes focused on my parted lips, flickering to my nipples which he so expertly teased, my flat belly peeking beyond the tangle of his arms, the hand beyond the fabric moving ever so slowly, deliberately, eliciting moans from my trembling body.

My body trembled at his touch. Unrelenting, revering each curve and swell, each mound and rise. His hands did not leave my body, tender touches of delightful torment. My chest heaved against his, my breath emerging in short sharp gasps.

"So fucking beautiful." He kissed my shoulder. His hands fell from my body and he spun me around. Our lips slammed together, my need desperate as I devoured his mouth. He pulled my legs up, and I wrapped myself around him as he walked over to the bed. Letting me slip from his grip, he set me on the edge and stood back admiring me.

I loved that about Leon, his unconditional attention, the look that said he appreciated everything he saw without a word ever spoken.

"Spread your legs for me Jane."

I wanted to, I tried to, but every instinct told me that there was a predator in the room, an animal masquerading as a gentleman. I clamped my thighs closed. Leon let out an agonised growl.

He began to unbutton his shirt. Dragging his piercing gaze across my body as he unbuttoned each button one at a time, slowly, methodically, self-assured. As his shirt fell open, he revealed at last what lay beneath.

His chest rose and fell unevenly beneath sloping shoulders. The steely contours of his abs as they narrowed at the hips where his suit pants clung to arched bones. A trail of black hair rounded his belly button and disappeared beyond the line of his boxers. I could see his erection as it pushed against the soft cotton.

He slipped out of his pants, but left the boxers on, teasing me with his secret.

"Spread your legs for me Jane."

"Make me."

He growled at me and lunged at the bed. I squealed scrambling backwards until my hands found the headboard. His heavy weight pinned me to the bed. His hands hooked around my wrists holding them above my head, forcing me to arch my back. His exquisite mouth found my hardening nipples. He feasted on my breasts, moving from one to the other, then back again, relentless. The mounting pleasure throbbing between my legs, craving release.

"Leon," I moaned his name, it was a plea.

For less.

For more.

For everything.

His mouth released me. "Spread your legs for me Jane." The hold on my wrists grew firmer as I complied at last. His hand slipped into my underwear and parted my lips, just hovering, not quite touching. I could feel the warmth of his fingers as his mouth returned to its earlier torment.

My body burned in desperate agony, I needed to be sated, satisfied, released, and yet Leon tormented me with his mouth, with his fingers. I strained my hips against his fingers, hot pleasure shot into my core. I repeated the action, the swelling delight built inside me as the edge came ever closer. My body quivered, the torment of my nipples, maddening, infuriating, delicious. I was close.

Leon pulled away his fingers and tongue, but his hands were yet to release mine. "You are sensational Jane." He kissed my shoulder, as I squirmed with need. "I am going to let go now, but I don't want you to move. If you do, I'll have to start all over again."

I nodded. Leon's wet, hot lips landed on mine, he bit my lower lip as he let go of my wrists. I remained still as his eyes swept along my body. He clasped the elastic band of the underwear and slipped it off my legs. I could hear a low rumble in his chest as he looked at my throbbing pussy. So needy for him.

He slipped off the bed and at last removed his boxers. His hard cock stood erect, the veins pulsed along it, straining. He slipped a condom on and stood at the edge of the bed.

His mouth peppered gentle kisses on my legs and thighs, my belly, my breasts, my neck and my mouth as he blanketed my body with his.

His hips thrust against my opening, and then he was inside me, filling me up. He held himself there and looked into my eyes. I could see the strain to remain composed, his need matched mine.

He pulled himself out and plunged into me again, shooting pleasure into my core, my hips rising to meet him. He repeated the action again, his rhythm was calculated and stirring, pushing me closer as I ground my body against his. His neck corded, his mouth a thin line, I could see the restraint falling away from him. His thrusts became less measured, but frantic and fast, slamming into me, I arched upward to take all of him as he pushed me over the edge. I exploded into a thousand pieces beneath him. Pleasure filled me, a hot fiery eruption as I called out his name. His hips pounded against me, and with a final shuddering release, his fingers dug into my flesh as he let out a husky primal growl.

He rolled away, and I lay breathless in his arms. My body quaking with delicious aftershocks. His strong arms winged around me, he kissed the top of my head as I listened to the rhythm of his heart.

There are pains that you don't mind. Like the aching muscles you wake up with after a long night. You don't mind the cramping sensations because every time you move, your mind rewinds to the moment of how you sustained this pain, and you smile and rub your thighs or arms or neck. I groaned in uncomfortable pleasure feeling the empty space beside me.

"Good morning sleepy head." He was in his boxers and nothing else. He was a vision. Tangled wild hair and a flashing smile that softened all his hard features. His steely contours fluid as he moved towards the bed. He planted a soft kiss on my lips. I moaned or groaned, half in pleasure and half in a sleepy stupor. How could he look so good this early in the morning?

"Breakfast?"

"Shower." My voice still scratched with sleep.

"Don't mind if I do." He followed me to the bathroom uninvited.

Despite the evening we had shared, I still felt nervous around him. Being naked around Leon was something I wanted to get used to, and he made it easy by removing his boxers. I might have sighed or gasped or done something to expel all the air from my lungs and attempted to suck it all back in. Leon pretended not to notice as he stepped into the shower and held the door open for me expectantly.

The oversized bathroom could have held half a football team. The hot water pelted my sore body, and then there were hands. Leon's lathered hands massaged my body, neck, back, feet and everything in between. He was gentle and sensuous, his hands gliding over me, finding their way to my breasts and between my legs.

"What are you doing to me?"

"Washing you." He grinned not hiding his satisfaction of his effects on me.

He dipped his head toward me, his lips finding mine, his kiss, deep and hungry. I curled my fingers around his cock and he let out a surprised gasp. I stroked his swelling erection, and he rewarded me with a choked moan.

"What are you doing?" he breathed through clenched teeth, his hips rocked, sliding in my grip.

"Washing you." I bit my lip as his rhythm sped up and his eyes rolled slightly upwards. Leon's breathing became louder, heavier.

"Stop." A scratched whisper.

"Make me," his eyes flashed at my dare. His hand landed against my wrist but he didn't yank it off, his hips still working against my hand. "You can make it up to me later."

His hand fell away. "Jane." He groaned against me, his hand clutching mine, guiding it, speeding up, pressing harder against his hardening shaft, his body began to shake like a tree in a hurricane, his mouth pulled back and his body twitched as he moaned his release.

Leon found my mouth. His tongue slipped inside and I could taste him. Even in the morning he tasted delicious, like a flavour that was made just for me. When he pulled away, he wrapped his arms around me holding me under the deluge of water. Letting the water wash away the rest of the soap.

After we had towelled off, he called the reception desk again informing them we were ready for our breakfast.

We sat across from one another, he nibbled on bacon and eggs, I sipped my coffee unable to tear myself away from his bare chest and intense chocolate eyes.

"I meant what I said last night."

"You said a lot of things." I toyed with him.

The scowl crossed his face just as I had predicted. "About wanting more. From you, with you."

I sipped on my coffee pretending my stomach didn't feel like a thousand fists were squeezing it. "What about Scott?"

"What about him?" Leon looked up from his plate and into my eyes.

"What would he think?"

"It's taken care of."

"What does that mean?" I straightened in my chair and put my cup down.

Leon sucked in a deep breath and let his fork drop. "When Scott sent you over to me, he knew I would never touch you, not as long as you worked for me. When you walked out of my office after that first day, I called him. We talked. Over the years he mentioned you more than once, how funny you were, how intelligent and fun. I already had a picture of you in my head well before I saw you. And then I did." His hands clenched for a second, as he leaned in across the table.

"You blew me away in an instant. You were not at all what I was expecting, and in many ways, I already knew you. I wanted you the second I laid eyes on you." I tried to remember how to breathe.

"I called Scott as soon as you were in the elevator, we had a conversation. He told me I wasn't allowed to have you, ever." Leon scoffed at the idea.

"He never told me that."

"Did he really have to?"

I let the question sink to the floor unanswered. We both knew the answer.

"I know you guys have become distant, him and his stupid games and you with your new career." He brushed a hand through his wet hair sweeping it to the side. "I called him yesterday, told him what my intentions were. He wasn't happy."

"You what?" there was so much more I wanted to say

about assumptions and presumptions and assholes, but Leon held up his hand.

"I told him that he's had two years. Two years to make a move, to try and pry you away from me, to try and claim you as his own, and yet all he did was sit at home and dream. He may have had some childhood crush, but I have suffered you. I have been agonised by desire, the need for you. I have earned my claim to you. I tried to keep my distance, I tried to keep my hands off and face turned the other way, but fuck Jane, you have completely destroyed me."

My heart bounded around my ribcage like a feral animal. My anger dissolved. "I'm still going to have to call him."

"I'd be surprised if you didn't."

"How pissed is he?"

"Let's just say I don't think he's going to be talking to me much."

I nodded and reached across the table putting my hand on his. "Are you OK?"

He gave me a wounded look. "About choosing you over my brother?"

I pursed my lips unsure of how to say yes.

Leon stood up and pulled me to him, his lips collided with mine like an asteroid hurtling on a path of destruction. His arms bound around me and he plunged his fingers into my hair. "It was never a choice for me Jane." He pecked my lips. "He'll come around." His lips found mine once more. I knew he only said it to appease me, but I didn't care. The way his body moved against mine, the way he was already leading us back to bed, ripping my robe open, searing heat through me. Falling to earth, hurtling towards the ground and slamming down with such devastating impact I knew I never had a choice either.

～

Having Leon was like having the best part of a natural disaster. Everything about him was over the top, big strong and utterly devastating.

My writing suddenly became happier, steamier than before. All of our shared nights and secrets became fodder for Gabriel and Mia.

Leon would leave work early and come over, completely disrupting my nights. He took me out dancing and to little dingy restaurants that were dark and small, where the food was delicious and where his hand was always on me, in me.

We laughed. It was a happy time, and for whatever reason, Gabriel barked and growled and brooded. Despite giving him Mia, he would never be satisfied. The more time I spent with Leon, the less time I needed to be with Gabriel.

I served him Mia on a silver platter. Naked and hot and wanting, ready for everything he had to give her and more, and yet all he wanted was me.

We were dating for almost three months the night that Sammy called him in and he had to rush back into work. Leon dropped me off, a guilty look on his face. I gave him a quick peck and told him to go.

When I walked inside Gabriel was waiting for me. He pushed me up against the wall, pinning me with his hips.

"I've been waiting for you Jane," he growled in a menacing tone. His hands rested on either side of my face, his mouth an inch away from mine.

"Not tonight Gabriel." I pushed his chest away. He did not budge, instead, grinding his hips against mine.

"Gabriel."

He didn't stop, his face dropped to my neck and he peppered it with soft, warm kisses. "Jane," he whispered my name as his lips rounded my chin and fell on my mouth. His kiss was feathery and gentle, while his hips, worked against mine. His tongue slipped into my mouth, the kiss suddenly hungry, savage, overpowering.

I felt his need. He felt my hesitation.

He pulled away.

"Is it him? Is that why you won't let me have you?"

I nodded, my body on fire.

"Do you love him?"

I pondered the question. Although I knew the answer. As did Gabriel. I saw the shadow cross his face.

"Gabriel," I stepped towards him as he retreated. My body tensed, I felt like I had to pry my jaw apart to speak. "Why can you not be content? I have given you Mia, she is everything you could want. She worships you. She lets you do all your dirty little things to her, she plays all your games and follows all your rules. So why can't you just be fucking happy Gabriel?"

His nostrils flared and his chest pushed up. "Because, she is not you." His beautiful jaw clenched and his eyes flashed.

Unrequited love. Except I did love him, but not in the same way I could love Leon. A flicker of an idea for my book set deep in my head and I pushed it away for later. I felt cold, bad, mean. But I couldn't control these impulses to write, to punish Gabriel in every way I could, just to have him crawl back and beg to worship me. It gave me a thrill.

"Gabriel." I reached for his hand, this time he let me take it as I placed it on my heart. "I will always love you."

"But not in the same way I love you." He stepped back letting my hand fall away, then disappeared down the hall.

I would have followed him but my phone rang. I saw Leon's name flash across the screen.

"Miss me already?"

"Like you won't believe." His husky undertone sent a shiver to my core. "But I can't make it back to yours tonight. I need to sort things out here."

"OK." I pouted.

"See you tomorrow sweet Jane."

"Bye."

I hung up disappointed. Throughout dinner, Leon teased me with a practised finger buried beneath the folds of my skirt. He enjoyed how my skin prickled with sweat and goosebumps. How my heart rate accelerated and my flesh turned pink, how I stumbled across words and swallowed hard. He would tease and pull away, tease and pull away. An evil delight, a devastating joy that left me hungry after food for satisfaction only he could provide.

Coming home to Gabriel's pulsing hips did nothing to relieve the throbbing that needed sating.

"Fuck it," I said to no one in particular and marched to my room. I found the red lingerie Leon bought for my birthday and pulled it on. I found a knee-high skirt that hugged my thighs and a low black singlet that revealed enough flesh in all the right places.

I could feel the driver's eyes on me while he wound around dark streets. It was almost closing time when I arrived at The Hot Bird.

Lefty sat on his high stool by the door, a quiet empty gateway. Noise spilt from inside. Dave must have been busy elsewhere.

Lefty stood up, a knowing grin spread across his face when he saw me.

"Hi." I could feel the flush creep across my face. Why did I come here? If I stepped inside, everyone would know why I was going upstairs. My courage left me.

"Evening Miss Miller, you look lovely."

"Thanks Lefty, but I think I'm going to go. I don't want to –"

"No need to worry Jane." Lefty cut me off and winked. "Right this way."

He stood up, his towering form casting a square shadow over me. He turned to the alley behind him and went to a door I had not noticed before. It was covered in graffiti and well camouflaged into the wall. Unless inspected from close up it seemed to be just part of the brickwork.

Lefty pulled out a bunch of heavy keys and flipped them around, sticking one into the hole and unlocking the door. It swung open easily and opened up to a staircase.

"His emergency exit," Lefty winked at me. "Third floor."

"Thank you," I beamed at the big man and turned to tackle the stairs in my high-heeled boots. They echoed as I climbed up to the third floor and pushed the door open. I was right by the elevator bay and again found myself surprised at never noticing the door. it sat in an identical frame to the panel on the other side. Without a handle or any marking, it looked like just another wall.

I didn't come to The Hot Bird to dissect the wonder of hidden doors and staircases and so I marched down the corridor to Leon's office. I could hear voices.

His voice.

"I don't give a shit how long it takes or what it costs Marco, fix it."

Why was he talking to Marco?

Marco. The big Italian man always surrounded by ten other men and the smell of spicy aftershave, that is meant to be expensive but smelled cheap. Marco that poured a pitcher of water on me and stood snivelling the next day asking for my forgiveness. Marco that pulled out a wad of cash the size that normal people don't carry around and tipped me $500 'for my trouble.' There was so much more I needed to know about Leon.

His back was turned to his door, but he saw my reflection in the large black windows. He whipped around his eyes falling on me, flashing with dark intention.

"I'll have to call you back." He didn't wait for an answer, just hung up and flung his phone on his desk.

"Sweet Jane." He pinned me with a savage glare, biting his lower lip. "What are you doing here?"

He hadn't moved. "I felt bad thinking of you working late all alone. I came to see if I could make your night better."

"Shit Jane, with you, dressed like that, I will never get any work done."

"I promise not to distract you." I bypassed him and went to sit on the single chair facing his desk crossing my legs, my hands folded across my knees.

Leon sucked in breath and crossed the room rounding his desk. He fell into his chair his eyes glued on me.

I let my hands fall from my knees and uncrossed them, spreading them casually allowing the skirt to hike up my thigh.

Leon dragged his eyes to his computer, tapping furiously on the keys. His eyes flickered over to me.

"Fuck Jane, I can't work like this, go sit somewhere else please." He took a galvanising breath and returned to his screen.

I stood up and walked to the drinks cart, making sure to swing my hips as I walked. These boots were not cheap and not comfortable and he was going to appreciate my efforts whether he liked it or not.

I threw a few ice cubes in a tumbler and poured some whiskey over them, they crackled gently against the glass. I walked over to Leon who was still pretending he wasn't watching my every move.

I sat on the corner of his desk pushing myself high enough so my thighs rested on the cold polished wood. I crossed my legs and placed the drink by my side.

Leon shot me a hungry look. "What are you doing Jane?"

"Just made you a drink. You seem stressed, thought it might help you relax."

He studied my face waiting for a twitch of my lips, for a glimpse of amusement. I held my face firm, I was going to give him nothing. I shifted, my skirt scaling higher on my thigh. Leon's eyes fell on the exposed flesh, taut and smooth.

Almost as if on autopilot, his hand began to stroke my exposed skin, warm and tingling.

He downed the drink in his tumbler and set it down, his eyes dancing with menace.

"Spread your legs Jane."

At last.

I let my legs fall apart for him. His fingers trailed the outside of my thighs and stroked my leg reaching for the elastic of my underwear. He yanked the delicate fabric and it tore away from my skin. He laced my booted legs through the red lingerie and tucked it into the breast pocket of his suit.

Air rushed between my legs, a delicate kiss of air on exposed skin that sent a thrill through me. I shivered with delight.

Excitement.

Trepidation.

I could sense Leon was not himself his brown eyes turbulent, dark.

He manoeuvred his chair, the wheels spinning, rounding my legs, his face came to rest between my knees. I could see his eyes focus on the apex of my legs. His eyes widened a fraction and he blew a long, measured breath. I shivered. He grinned and grabbed my thighs parting them wider. I gasped.

Leon opened his top drawer and pulled out the coil of lace that he used to wrap up my birthday presents.

He bit his lip and gave me a long, considered look.

"You are a distraction sweet Jane." He stood up. "But not an unwelcome one." He sucked in a long breath and pushed away items on his desk creating an empty space. His voice was strained and heavy. I remained silent.

"Lie back Jane."

My body settled back against the cold hardness of his

white desk. The cold settled on my skin like an invisible blanket. It tickled and licked at my flesh, my nipples hardened from the seeping heat, and yet I was burning with anticipation.

"Hands over your head Jane."

Leon rounded the desk and took my wrists in his hands tugging them lightly. "Do you trust me Jane?"

"Yes." I shivered beneath his touch. How could I not? He had waited for two years. He had kept all his promises. Of course, I trusted him.

He tugged at my wrists again, stretching my body against his table. The lace felt soft against my skin as he weaved it around my wrists, binding them together then pulling the lace through. Leon's fingers worked quickly as he tied the other end to the leg of his desk the rest of the coil falling away, rolling to the floor. He tugged at the lace extending me, restraining me.

Leon stood up, his eyes gleamed with wickedness as they trailed my body. "You look fucking amazing Jane." I quivered, his face bent over mine. His lips capturing mine, devouring me.

He rounded the table once more and grabbed my knees prying them further apart. Exposing me, his eyes burning into me. My body tingled with anticipation.

The first kiss sent a shiver up my spine, his hot fingers brushed my cold thighs lifting my hips off the chilly table, warming me with their touch.

Leon leisurely kissed the inside of my legs, edging his way toward my inner thighs, revering every inch of skin, with his thick, full lips and hot, wet tongue. His whiskers scratching my skin. His mouth hovered around the apex of my legs, his breath the calm before the storm.

His tongue found my slit and he licked me languidly, slowly. I struggled against his restraints and he pulled away eliciting a moan from me. I craned my neck trying to lift myself off the table, to see his face.

He met my gaze and readjusted my skirt. "You look so pretty when you squirm, my sweet, sweet Jane." He licked his lips and smiled wickedly at me.

"Do you trust me Jane?"

"Yes." I whimpered, I needed his touch.

He stalked around the table and pulled on the hem of my shirt lifting it over my face, letting it come to rest over my eyes.

The world went dark.

I swallowed hard.

"Don't move." His voice a warm whisper by my ear, my stomach coiled, a bag of snakes slithering on my inside.

For a moment there was silence. I could hear my heart hammering in my chest, my ragged breaths, the soft thud of his shoes on carpet.

I squealed at his hands as they traced my waist, trailing to my bra where he pushed each breast out of its cup, my nipples pinching at the cold air.

The silence engulfed me as I lay exposed, vulnerable and totally, completely drenched.

"Fuck Jane," he murmured from somewhere above me.

I took a galvanising breath. I could smell his aftershave and the mild hint of peppermint that followed him around like his shadow. I felt his body heat as he bent over my body seconds before his hot mouth closed around a nipple, his tongue whirled around me, as I writhed under his touch.

The heat disappeared. The silence broken by the jingle of ice. The thump of the tumbler reset on the table, and his heat was back. His mouth at my nipple, freezing and wet. The ice cube danced around in his mouth my nipple pinching against his assault. The ice trail ended at my belly button where the cube felt heavy and foreign. Leon traced the cold path he had just carved with his tongue, returning warmth, eliciting moan after moan with delicious torture.

Leon left the ice cube in my belly button. I could feel the weight of it was almost gone. He pulled away for a second, then his hands were at my skirt, pulling up the fabric, exposing me. And there he was again between my legs, his tongue whirling and sucking, fracturing my sanity. I quivered beneath him as he brought me closer to the edge, the dark forcing me to feel everything. I struggled against the restraints wanting to brush my fingers through his hair, wanting to push his head against me, grind against him.

His fingers dug into my thighs forcing me down, forcing me open. Leaving me completely at his mercy. But he showed none. Aching bliss set in, as exquisite pleasure built, craving release. He freed my hips allowing me to move. His fingers found their way inside me eliciting a wave of ecstasy. With a shuddering, clenching spasm it took me, a frenzied explosion of exquisite sensation. Leon remained, milking from me wave after wave of glorious splendour allowing my body to crash against great, shuddering, clenching spasms.

He pulled away. I could hear the soft thud of his feet as he rounded me.

"Exquisite," he murmured in my ear, his mouth found my lips and kissed me soft and gentle. The kiss was long and deep. When he pulled away my hands were free of the table though my wrists were still bound. Leon peeled the shirt from my eyes so that I could see him.

His naked form was beautiful. Carved by the gods themselves, every curve and crevice magnificent in its own right. Almost noble. His strong arms lifted me from the table and winged around me, flooding me with warmth. He turned me around.

"Bend over for me Jane." His voice was smooth and reassuring at my ear.

I gripped the lip of his desk, my feet planted on the carpet. He sucked in an appreciative breath.

"Fuck Jane," he purred as he lifted my skirt over my ass.

His body folded against mine as he thrust himself inside me. Gripping onto my hips he pounded into me, his breathing heavy. He did not need long. His body jerked and bucked as he moaned and shuddered. His heavy body blanketing mine as he caught his breath.

When he had regained himself, he kissed my shoulder and reached for my wrists releasing me from my binds.

"Thank you," Leon whispered in my ear pulling away from me.

"For what?"

"For trusting me." He lay another kiss on my shoulder and pulled away disappearing into his bathroom.

I pushed away from the desk and stretched my hands, my shoulders sore and strained. I heard the taps come to life in the bathroom and followed him in.

He stood halfway in the shower testing the water, two towels already out waiting for us to finish what we hadn't even started.

We stood under the water knowing what would come next. Leon closed the distance between us and kissed me. Needy and desperate, somehow forlorn. I threw my arms around him, comforting whatever demon he was fighting.

"I love you sweet Jane."

"I love you too Leon."

He made love to me then, soft and gentle like a man starved. Filling me up and breaking me open. "I love you Jane," he whispered again and again before release found us both.

When we had towelled and dressed, he handed me my trench coat. "What are you doing?"

"I'll have Lefty take you home. He's been waiting."

A flood of heat trickled to my face. "What? Why?"

He cupped my face in his hands and kissed me. "Tonight has been magnificent Jane, but I still have to work. I need to sort out this mess before tomorrow."

"What mess?"

"I'll tell you in the morning, I promise, but please go now."

I shot him a look of dissatisfaction, but he held his hands up in surrender, his mouth curled into a pout and his eyebrows creased in a soft V.

I sighed and crossed my arms. "Fine, but I'm not happy about it."

"Really? I couldn't tell." His lip curled up into a grin, I huffed in retort. Brilliant I know.

He picked up the phone from his desk and dialled. "You can come up now." He hung up unceremoniously.

I heard the elevator ping and clenched my jaw. I really didn't want to go. Leon kissed me once more. Tender, intoxicating.

"I love you," he whispered in my ear releasing me, leaving behind a hint of peppermint and a gaping hole.

The car ride was silent. I could barely look at the man, he knew I had come to throw myself at Leon, and that Leon had given me exactly what I asked for. I looked out of the window and relived the last few hours in my head.

"We're here miss Jane."

"Thanks Lefty, I appreciate the ride."

He saluted with a single finger. The car remained idle until I closed the door of the building behind me. Waiting for the elevator I heard the whine of his engine pulling away.

I crawled into bed, exhaustion pulling me into its sweet caress.

"Where have you been?" Gabriel's scowl was beautiful and frightening.

"You know where I was."

"Why didn't you stay? He said he loved you Jane then threw you away."

"No, he didn't, he had to work."

"Sure he did. If you call him now would he pick up?"

"He's busy, Gabriel, just drop it."

"I would never throw you away Jane."

In life much like in books, you should never really get comfortable, never complacent for you never know what's going to happen next. You think your character has found their ideal job, partner, friend, pet and then BAM out of left field the carpet gets pulled right from under them, and everything that was so perfect a moment ago lays shattered in a million pieces by their feet.

Now if you think I am being overly dramatic, you may be right, but life can be brutal and cruel and I felt that she was taking out her anger on me.

I was sitting with Gabriel going over pages. Despite waking late, I felt tired. Like I hadn't slept at all. My body still bore the marks of my night with Leon, my shoulders ached and stung with movement, my legs felt heavy. My hands strained and my fingernails stained. But the rest of me felt giddy and excited for something new.

Gabriel seemed calmer that morning. Pleasant even. Ever since Leon came into my life Gabriel was like a man with his back up against the wall. I leaned against his chest and we read. I could feel Gabriel's roaming hands, the thoughts at the end of his fingers. I didn't push him away. I should have, but I had been rejecting him for so long over Leon, that it was just nice to have him so relaxed around me.

The phone sounded shrill in the apartment. Like that bell that saves you from something. I got up, leaving Gabriel on the couch, pouting with a mock sad face.

"I have to get it, it's Sammy." I didn't have to get it but I wanted to. I hadn't heard from her in weeks and I missed her. Over my time at The Hot Bird she was like a big sister to me, not working with her anymore had left a gap even Leon's big cock and giant personality couldn't fill.

"Sammy." I smiled into the phone.

The silence was odd and I felt the shiver as it ran down my spine. Maybe I sensed it before I heard the snivel. Maybe it was the silence or the way the air quivered around it.

"Sammy?" I could feel the earth shift slightly, my stomach coiled.

"Jane." Her voice shook, my stomach churned in response.

"Sammy, you're scaring me, what's happened?"

"You haven't heard?"

"Sammy." Gabriel shot me a concerned look from the couch but didn't get up.

"Jane. It's Leon." I could feel the room spin. "There was an accident." The air squeezes out of my lungs, the room felt smaller as I reached blindly for a wall.

"How bad is it?" my chest heaved, my breath sharp and heavy as my lungs struggled for air.

"Jane, sweetheart." My throat constricted. "He's gone."

The phone fell from my hand in slow motion, I could hear her voice calling to me, distant and strange. Bile rose to my throat. I clutched my stomach trying to hold the bottom from falling out, but it was too late, it had just fallen from beneath my feet and the rest of my body followed.

I'm not sure when Gabriel arrived, but his strong hands wrapped around my shoulders.

"Jane?"

"Leon," I whispered, hot tears stinging my face. Gabriel's hands stiffened around me for just a second and he kissed my forehead.

"It's OK Jane, I'm still here." He wrapped his hands around me, closing in on me like a lid to a crypt, sealing me in darkness and despair.

"I don't want you to be here, I want Leon." I pounded on his shoulders as he held me tighter still.

"I know you don't mean that Janey. That's just the anger talking. It's all right, it'll be alright."

I had no more words, just tears that fell to the floor like the broken parts of me.

~

W hen I woke up the world was still bleak and black. Every muscle ached and screamed. My body felt heavy, weighed down by deep-set grief that swallowed me whole.

Despite Gabriel's attempts, I did not get out of bed for almost a week. Food was a foreign concept as was the shower. I think there may have been some concerned people at the door a few times, but it's true what they say, if you ignore them long enough, they go away.

"Would you like to get up today?" Gabriel's words were sweet, but I could feel the sour undertone beneath. He had been practically dancing around the apartment knowing Leon was out of our lives while I sat in my dark pit my entire universe collapsed.

Leon was going to be my home. I felt it. I felt it under my skin, in the very sinew of my being, with every beat of my heart and now that same heart lay in pieces, like a mixed-up puzzle with too many parts. I didn't know where to start rebuilding. I didn't know that I wanted to.

Voices came from the corridor, I heard my door and a baritone, followed by the sweet sing-song of Grish.

"I am in your apartment Jane, I am coming inside."

I pulled the blanket over my head and rolled onto my side curling up into a tight ball. I didn't want him here. I didn't want anyone here.

"Jane." His voice was closer, he must have been at the door. "Jane, today you must get up."

I ignored him, he would go away, it worked with everyone else.

Well almost everyone else.

"Jane, you need to get up and go shower."

"I think he's serious." Gabriel's elated voice whispered in my ear. I swatted him away.

"Jane. You will get up. Now." The room was flooded with light, my blanket suddenly shining. I groaned, tucking my knees into my chest, holding the pain and tears at bay. If I moved, it would all spill out. Again.

"Jane. You must get up today."

"Why?" I moaned from beneath the blanket.

"Because." His voice became softer, affectionate even. "Today is your last chance to say goodbye."

The funeral.

Already.

Had it been seven days? Seven days of darkness and oblivion.

"You must get up and say goodbye."

I uncurled my body and poked my head out. I nodded. I wasn't going to get up alone.

Grish held out his hand, despite his best efforts to adopt me as a third child of sorts he had always remained stiff around me, alert. Today was no exception. I held on to his hand as if it was the only thing that kept me from falling over the precipice. My knuckles white against his cinnamon skin.

We took small steps, Grish led me to the bathroom. He sat me on the toilet seat and turned on the water to my shower. He adjusted the taps and looked at me woefully. "Shower, get clean. I'll be right outside."

The stinging water splashed on my face, washing away days of sweat and tears, covering up new ones that erupted from me. My body shook against the cold tiles as I gasped for breath. My mind swinging back and forth from today to our first date. It should have been Leon's hands washing me.

"I can do that for you if you like." Gabriel entered the shower.

"Just go away." I turned my back to him. When I turned back, he had left.

I walked out of the bathroom and my stomach croaked as I smelled the fresh aroma of coffee and eggs, I'm sure there was toast as well. If I wasn't the neighbour of the only vegetarian in the building, I bet there would have been bacon too.

I dressed. It was a slow and agonising process. It wasn't that I was confused about what to wear. It was the heaviness, the dead arms and legs that refused to let me live. To let me get on with things.

I thought I wouldn't be able to eat, but I did, I was famished. The food threatened to come up as soon as I had finished it. Maybe it was the coffee that Grish made despite his aversion to the stuff, or maybe it was his sing-song reassurances that helped me keep it down. Keep everything down. Keep it all together.

Grish took me to the church. The first person I saw was Scott. I knew he was still angry at me. The look he gave me was less than friendly. I wanted to say how sorry I was, how much I missed his brother, how much I missed them both. Instead, I waited like a coward until he turned his back to me and made his way inside, his parents on either side of him.

I hoped Sammy would rescue me, wrap her arms around me and comfort me in that way only big sisters could.

Her hug was cold and distant as if we were strangers. Sammy looked me up and down, seemingly perplexed as if she was trying, just like me, to piece together a great big puzzle. I let it go putting it down to her grief.

Grish remained by my side throughout the funeral. The grip on my hand tightened, as I cried silently when the earth hit the wooden coffin with a sudden and terrifying thud.

It was all so final.

The police determined foul play. The brake wires of his car were cut. Was he coming to see me when he didn't stop at the red traffic light? They were looking into some underworld figures Leon was associated with.

Marco.

My heart leapt to the same conclusion as my head.

It would be two years before Leon's case was solved and two years before I saw any of those people again.

My recovery was slow and agonising, but where my heart suffered my writing flourished. My next two books were dark and bitter. Gabriel and Mia suffered loss after devastating loss and my readers lapped it up, loving the heart-shredding agony I dragged them through.

Gabriel brooded a lot. His desire for me was insatiable, and I denied him time and again. His anger sat on the surface like a shimmering mirage. I could not understand his rage. But I used it against him, against Mia and my audience loved it.

Despite the tragedy, the pain, the brooding and agonising, Gabriel was always there. Comforting, soothing, reminding me every day of his presence. After the eighth month of mourning, I woke to find that the darkened veil that had covered my life had lifted, slowly. The pain and heartbreak simmered to something close to bearable and I could breathe again. Smile and laugh, and open myself up once more. To life, to love, to Gabriel.

2005

The restaurant was somewhere I would have never picked. Not because the music was lame or the waiters looked like penguins with carrots up their arses. Not even because of the over the top decor and golden cutlery. It was definitely the food.

When they placed the bite-sized portions before us, my mouth dropped and my belly grumbled for the fourth time that night. I saw Björn's face drop when he heard it again. I had no control over my face and suspect it pulled in many directions all at once but not in the happy kind of way where you only use like three muscles to smile with.

I tried smiling. I could feel the effort I was putting into it, I'm sure he saw it too.

Björn reached for my hand. A low growl came from across the table. I ignored Gabriel who had been sitting like a third wheel throughout the meal, eavesdropping and being generally annoying.

Gabriel grew morose and threatening over the last six months. With his potential death or happily ever after, and my promise to Björn to move on to a fresh series, his mood had soured daily. It didn't help that I refused his every attempt to touch me. I didn't need his dick, his tongue, him.

I think somewhere I hoped that pushing Gabriel away would give him the freedom to leave, to go and be happy, perhaps in another place where Mia existed too. I had made my choice. I chose Björn.

Björn looked into my eyes squeezing my hand gently. "Where did you go?"

"Nowhere."

"Sorry about the food, the place came highly recommended, and I wanted tonight to be special."

I raised an eyebrow. "Special? Why?"

"Well." He cleared his throat, his usually stoic manner fractured by beads of nervousness that peppered his forehead and made his lip twitch. I could see his knee bouncing at a hundred miles per hour. I liked that he was nervous like this, vulnerable, needy. It made me feel like I needed to wrap myself around him and reassure him.

"It's our anniversary today."

My face did that oh fuck face. You know the one, the one where you think you've forgotten something really important and your face stretches back against itself in a grimace tainted by sheer panic. "What anniversary?" I could hear the nervousness in my voice.

His face burst into an amused smile. "Relax Jane. It's just been six months since you made me take a day off work."

"How romantic." My sarcasm was as thick as the zabaglione.

His smile just widened in response. "Oh Jane. I am not making myself clear. Maybe it's because you make me so nervous."

"Nervous? You?"

"Every day."

"I'm not sure how I should be taking this."

My humour was tainted with anger, was he making fun of me?

Björn released my hand long enough to be able to run his own through that wild mop of his, that dangled and bounced around his fingers, making my own twitch.

"Jane. All I mean to say is that since the day you came knocking on my door all huffing and puffing and looking incredibly sexy with your red face and dark eyes, I have thought of nothing else but you. The way you've made me feel in the last six months has been incredible. Everything you touch it turns to magic. Jane, you make everything better."

I could feel the heat rise to my ears and drop to my core, as he continued. "You make everything better, food, conversation, sex, even watching TV. I just…" He sucked in a deep breath as if preparing himself. His eyes found mine, the hot blue fire was smouldering in the furnace of his stare. Fire scorching my resistance, melting my insides with desire and untold dirty things.

"I love you Jane Miller."

I gasped, sucking in the warmth of his words, as Gabriel roared, baring his teeth, his chest heaving, fists curled into white tight balls.

I found Gabriel's eyes for a second as I whispered the words, "I love you too."

Björn Captured my lips in his, a soft pillowy kiss full of promise and delight. There was nothing more than the tenderness of words shared.

I could feel the sickly-sweet feeling of being wanted as It wrapped its tentacles around me. I could feel the warmth as it spread around my body, splitting my face into an absurd smile that would linger, as Björn took me by the hand and pulled me away from the table. It would linger as he led me to his car. It lingered as we drove home, his hand on my thigh climbing ever higher, teasing promising but leaving me wanting. It lingered as we ascended the lift to the 37th floor.

But as he pushed me from the door, there would be no more smiling.

I could already feel the heat in the elevator, it closed in on us as we stood hand in hand. I could feel the tension in his body. Stiff and ready. But he waited. Jaw clenched, hands sweaty. He waited.

He waited until the elevator came to a smooth stop and the ping echoed in the deserted hallway that separated our doors by fifteen steps.

Björn yanked on my arm and slammed my body against the cold window pane that overlooked the city and allowed moonlight to saturate the hallway.

His hands curled into my hair and he clenched his fist around a clump of it, forcing my head up. His vulnerability gone, only pure unadulterated need left behind.

His lips crashed into mine in a long blistering kiss.

His burning body pushed mine against the cold pane, fire and ice.

He released my mouth, his eyes pinning me. While his free hand found its way under my shirt, his hot fingers trailing my skin, tracing the line of my ribs, finding their way to my bra.

Unceremoniously he pulled it up releasing my breasts. His hands kneading my flesh, his fingers finding my hardening nipples, tweaking, pulling teasing.

"Björn…" I whispered, my lips ached for his, just out of reach. He tugged my hair, forcing my eyes to lock onto his as he wreaked havoc on my throbbing aching breasts. My body craved him, needed him, his touch forcing his name from my lips.

He went to work on the other breast, my hips needing to grind against him. His body a steel immovable rod against me.

"Björn please…" I licked my lips, needing him to take me, and still, he refused. His hand leaving my breasts and indulging itself in a journey down. His finger slid under my skirt, gliding along my thigh. They found the elastic of my underwear. Björn's fingers expertly pushed the fabric away to one side, sweeping against my wetness.

I shuddered against him, and a hint of a smile wrinkled his fiery eyes.

Again he brushed against me eliciting a desperate, hungry moan from me.

Yearning to move, my body ached for release, as his fingers sparked need and desire from me. I longed for his body.

For release.

For more.

I groaned again, as teasing fingers got me ever closer.

"I'm going to let you go now Jane." Björn's accent thicker with lust, "I love you like this, all wild and hot."

I whimpered in response as his hand released my hair. And his body moved away from mine.

"You slut," came Gabriele's hiss in my ear. I was wondering when he would show up.

I ignored him. Anger didn't have a place here, not now.

Björn fell to his knees and yanked my skirt and underpants from me. My bare ass, cold against the window panes.

His tongue found my slit, shooting heat right to my core. I groaned for him, the pleasure building as his tongue flicked around me, tasting, devouring, teasing.

"Please, Björn." My legs shook as the edge drew ever closer.

Nearer.

My vision narrowed, till a building pulsing moment of release overtook me, the climax burning me to a cinder on a blue heat. I cried out my pleasure as wave after wave overtook me.

Björn stood up, I don't know when he undid his pants, but they pooled around his feet, his cock erect and twitching, needing a hole to fill. His hands tugged at the hem of my shirt and he pulled the fabric from me, ripping at the bra straps. He disposed of the clothes with a wayward throw.

His heat scorching me, the cold glass a soothing balm to the inferno inside.

Björn bent down, his cock found my opening and he thrust himself inside me with a groan. He stood to his full height, and I wrapped my legs around his strong hips. He crushed me to the window. His hips moving, burying himself deeper and deeper with each slow measured stroke. His head nestled in my chest his mouth tasting my nipples, as he pulsed into me, biting, sucking, thrusting, fucking.

My body forgot how to breathe, as I gasped for air. Need and pleasure built inside me as Björn moved. Grinding against me, thrusting me beyond the window into a land of pleasure so intense, I felt I may cry.

He pumped his hips, his breath ragged and hot, his eyes strained and heated. Darkness took me again with a final glorious moment of ecstasy, I exploded around him. I cried out my pleasure clutching onto his back, fingers digging into pliable rock. Björn pumped furiously into me, and with a final jerk, he wrapped his hands around my back pulling me onto him, as if he needed to be even deeper. The echoes of my orgasm milking him as he moaned, abandoning himself to pleasure.

With ragged breaths he leant against me, his heavy body holding us both up.

He pulled away, his eyes now a simmering flame. "I love you Jane Miller," he whispered into my ear, and kissed my cheek gently.

"I love you too." Before his lips captured mine. The kiss was gentle and tender, and completely devastating.

Björn picked me up and released himself from me. His

eyes explored my nudity. His tongue flickered over his top lip and I could see the twitch of his cock.

"Let me make love to you Jane," he crooned.

"Make love to me? I thought you just did?" my eyebrow rose.

"No. I fucked you because you are mine. Now let me make love to you." He pulled his pants up, pulling up the zip not bothering with the belt and button as if they would just get in the way. With a swift move, he pulled me into his arms and lifted me like a bride on her wedding day. He carried me to my apartment, my clothes strewn along the path like fallen soldiers after a battle.

Björn pushed the door open and walked directly to my bedroom where he lay me on the soft mattress. The warmth and silkiness a stark contrast to the cold window.

He towered above the bed, watching my body, tracing each curve and dip with his eyes as he slowly peeled his clothes off.

"You can't do this Jane, you don't love him." I pushed Gabriel's voice away. I could see him, in the corner. He stood with a pained, broken expression.

Tomorrow I would write the final chapter of his book and set him free, but tonight Björn was going to make love to me.

He unbuttoned his shirt and it fell open revealing his broad chest, peppered with light hair, the corrugated flat of his abdomen and the ripples of muscles across his ribs. Björn's body flexed and stretched as he undid his pants and let them fall by his feet. Allowing my eyes to travel the length of his strong, thick thighs.

He stepped to the end of the bed and his body folded over mine. My heart throbbed as he leaned down to kiss me, his mouth capturing me in a sweet delicate kiss. He pulled away, trailing soft kisses along my body. Revering every inch of me, with delicate fingers and silky languid kisses. His tongue flicked over my achingly swollen breasts, he moaned in appreciation as I arched my back for him, giving full access to all I had to offer. Lingering warmth seduced me as he kissed his way down, I squirmed beneath his tongue, sensitive and needy once more as he left a single scorching kiss between my legs.

When he climbed above me, his lips shone and I could taste myself on him. His eyes hooded, framed by the shock of sweaty thick hair. He smiled, a sweet happy smile and then he eased himself into me.

"Jane." My name was lost in a groan.

With slow measured thrusts, he pushed himself deeper into me, his eyes focused on my face, his body burying itself into mine as if we were one, slamming into me, forcing pleasure from my lips, forcing quivers from my body, forcing heat to my core.

His thrusts sped up, his need growing as my hips answered his, pushing and grinding. My heart thrashed in my chest as I moaned my pleasure. Seized by a rush of sensation so intense, my body clung to his. A chain of spasms washed over me, as Björn grunted something unintelligible. I could feel the jerk of his body, as his hands squeezed my waist, pulling me, deeper,

lower,

grinding,

pulsing,

exhaling.

Collapsing.

Side by side we lay, two hearts breathing, entwined, strumming to a new beat. But there was a third heart in the room, and its beat was out of rhythm, its beat was angry and jealous radiating a green wave which ricocheted across the walls. I could feel his heartbeat just as much as I could feel mine and Björn's. The beat was like a familiar tune, something I may have heard once before, and for a second, I thought of Josh and Barry and Leon.

They all loved me too.

They left me too.

Before I could drown in thoughts of the past, Björn gathered me into him, he lay a gentle kiss on my shoulder as he curled his body around mine.

"I love you Jane Miller."

"I love you too," I said my eyes landing on Gabriel.

I didn't remember falling asleep. But sleep would have been better than waking up like this.

The room felt chilly. Not much had changed since I had fallen asleep in Bjorn's arms and yet it felt colder, darker, the night light dim against the harsh darkness that loomed outside.

I could feel the other body in the bed but it felt different, stiff, heavy. A cold shiver ran through me and for a second, I thought of terrified blue eyes, surprised, tortured, so very, very real.

I shot up. Or was I already sitting? The room spun around me. My hands felt sticky, my body wet. A cold shudder ran down my spine as I turned to Björn.

He was gurgling, panting, clutching his neck that spewed hot dark liquid.

"Jane," his strangled breath called for me, his eyes wide with terror.

"Björn," I screamed as I took the sight in.

His neck was slashed from ear to ear, the blood flowing from him in a dark, endless tidal wave, while he gurgled and splattered.

"Jane," he called to me in whispers, blood trickled from his broken lip.

I grabbed the sheet bunching it around his gaping neck. His arms flailed around me.

"Stop, I'm trying to help you." My voice was strangled, hot tears ran down my cheeks. Björn's arms grasping at mine, weak as the colour drained from his face. "Hang on, don't leave me," I cried.

Björn's breath became shallow, erratic, his body heaved as his lungs fought for air. He looked like a fish out of water, flailing, dying. His hand jerked, the blue fire of his eyes freezing over. With a final twitch, he was still. The blood oozed from his throat, the flood slowing to a steady stream.

"No! Björn!" I called for him, my hands still clenched around his neck trying to stem the endless flow that poured through my fingers and pooled onto the bed.

What the fuck just happened?

Teary eyed, I searched the room. It was then that I saw him. He was standing shirtless next to the bed a crazed satisfied look across his face. The knife dangled from his right hand, his torso and chin bathed in blood, his arm stained in red.

"Gabriel? What. Did. You. Do?" a glacial pang of pain like the stab of an icy dagger pierced my heart.

"Jane." He turned to me, his teeth gleaming in the soft light, his eyes softening. "I've taken care of it. You don't have to be afraid anymore."

"What are you talking about?"

"You're safe now Janey."

"Gabriel, what did you do?"

"I saved you."

My heart turned numb, black filled the edges of my vision as anger and fear flared inside me.

I leapt across the bed; my blood-stained hands heavy with the smell of metal. I reached for my notebook and a pen and tore the book open.

My shivering hand began to scribble, words forming in

squiggly unrecognisable writing, stained in blood as it stuck to the paper. My breath came in ragged, shallow gasps.

"What are you doing Jane?" his voice no longer warm and soothing.

"What I should have done a long time ago." My own voice quivered under tears.

"Put the pen down!" His voice was menacing as he prowled toward me, the knife back in his hand, where I needed it to be.

Gabriel clutched the knife in his blood-stained hands. A single tear marring his beautiful face. A world without her is no world at all.

"Jane, stop it now! You don't know what you're doing."

Collapsing to the floor, Gabriel turned the knife to his chest clutching it with two hands, the sharp edge hovering above his heart. Or where his heart used to be. The space now felt like an empty cavity.

He fought the knife as he crawled toward me, the knife to his heart, he managed to fall by my feet.

"Jane-"

He grabbed my leg and pulled. I fell to the floor the pen rolling from my hands. I kicked at his hand and crawled for the pen, my fingers brushing the edge.

Gabriel clawed my ankle pulling me toward him. With an agonising stretch, I reached for the pen.

Gabriel rolled me over, his weight pinning me to the floor. We panted. My chest heavy with sadness and effort. Even as he sat above me, I could appreciate his beauty. His flawless face twisted in agony, searing my soul.

"Jane, don't do this." The cords of his neck stretched taut.

My hand moved of its own accord, the words constricting my chest.

With a final brutal shove, Gabriel plunged the knife into his chest where it sank through skin and soft flesh, ripping through muscle, meniscus and tissue so that he could pierce the only part of him that ached.

Gabriel screamed in agony, clutching his chest, he struggled for breath. The searing pain in my heart spread like wildfire, Gabriel's shrieks, suddenly my own, as the knife protruded from my chest. I gripped the wooden knife handle lodged firmly into my body. I could taste metal in my mouth as howling screams drowned the room. I could feel the warmth of blood as it oozed gently from my wound.

Gabriel lay on the floor beside me, guttural chokes brought up bloodied spittle that leaked from his mouth.

He reached his hand to me and held it.

The world went black.

The first thing I felt was cold followed by intense white pain. The room was unfamiliar and shadows lurked around the bed, murmur of conversation drifted in broken chords around me. My mouth felt dry, like I had been licking cotton balls.

I coughed trying to swallow and my stomach turned. Nausea washed over me and I tried to pull my hand to my mouth. It was then I realised it was restrained. It did not feel cold like I would imagine handcuffs to be, but rather a cushioned restraint the ran the length of my wrist.

What the fuck was going on?

The shadows jerked at my movements. Blotted bodies becoming clearer around the edges as two men peered at me. One, dark and neat with hardened brown eyes, and the other, wild and pale with spectacled pale blue eyes.

"You're awake." The pale blue eyes smiled through glass, and the rest of the man came into focus. Silver hair in unruly strands framed his creased face.

"Where am I?" My voice scratched through my acrid throat.

"ICU," the man said as casually as ever.

"Where is Björn?"

The two men exchanged a look, the darker of the two, remaining stoic. "There was nothing we could do for him."

My heart squeezed and I flailed, the pain unbearable.

"Looks like the drugs are wearing off, I'll get one of the nurses to come in and help you with that."

"Wait…" it was a whisper, my lips parted mutely as the two figures disappeared.

The day blurred into nurses and jelly in cups and whispered conversation. The one constant was the figure that lurked by my bed, dark and silent he stood, like a sentinel. But I was yet to determine if he was there to protect me or protect everyone else from me.

The following day the flood gates opened. A flood of information that drowned me even as I tried to fight my way to the surface of it.

The surgeon, who eventually introduced himself as Doctor Clifford, kept saying how lucky I was to be alive and that if it wasn't for his brilliant handy work, I would have been dead. I was a miracle. A miracle that the blade missed my heart by a mere two millimetres.

A hair's breadth.

Dr Clifford spoke more about himself and his accomplishments during my surgery, than he did about my injury.

I felt numb.

I wished my heart had been pierced through. I wished for death. I remembered the vacant look in Björn's eyes as he scratched at my hand. I swore I was trying to help him. I recalled Gabriel's agonised screams as I shoved the blade into his heart, my heart?

I lost both the men I loved on the same night and somehow, I was responsible for murdering them both. I would stand trial for one, while the world would never know about the other.

When the doctor had gone, assuring me I would make a

swift and sound recovery, two policemen walked in in his stead. They filed into the room and proceeded to read me my rights explaining I was under arrest for the murder of Björn Hellström.

As they spoke, I felt my body flooding with adrenalin, my veins burning with liquid ice as my pounding heart forced it around my body. I wanted to run, to flee, but of course I wouldn't, if my restrains couldn't hold me down my injury would. They were talking about lawyers and rights to speak or not and I felt my body erupt in cold sweat, my fingers curled into a fist, nails digging into my palm. They asked me if I understood, and I wanted to answer except that I couldn't breathe. Fear clenched my lungs and squeezed, I was choking on the very thing that was keeping me alive.

"Just take a deep breath Jane." His voice carried through the beeping and shouting, through rough hands shaking me and a shrill voice screaming in indignation like a nun telling off a naughty child.

"You're here? I killed you."

"No Jane, now breathe." Gabriel smiled at me, filling me with warmth, love, relief.

It was the nurse that spoke next, "Are you alright darling?"

I nodded at her kind eyes and soft features.

"You two need to leave." She straightened up and faced the officers.

"We need to finish this arrest."

"Well she needs to rest." Her foot was tapping on the floor as they stood eyes glued to one another like gunslingers.

"She needs to confirm that she understands and we can leave." The taller of the two men stood firm.

The nurse turned back to me. The lines on her weather-beaten face smoothed as she bent down and brushed hair from my face. "Did you understand what they said darling?"

I nodded. Or I'm pretty sure I did, as she straightened out and glared at the men. "There you go then, she understands."

They grumbled a response and shuffled out of the room but not before reminding me of the guard that would be stationed outside my room until further notice.

The days that followed were a blur. Clarice organised a hotshot lawyer. Helen Ying. She was bigger than her small stature in all aspects of the law. Her commanding presence and tight pressed lips got everyone's attention. Her immaculate business suits clung to her body like the corporate skin it was, and it reeked of success and incited fear where necessary.

She gave me the gag order.

"Talk to no one, say nothing. You have now been arrested, but due to your health you will remain here until you are deemed well enough to be booked and go to a cell." Her eyes glazed over as she spoke as if the speech was coming from somewhere deep inside, some place so familiar she didn't have to be present in the room while she explained procedures. I'm fairly sure that after five minutes my face mirrored hers. Once she was done with the *basics* as she called them, she produced her phone and explained that she would be recording our conversation and that we needed to get down to business.

That first conversation was the hardest of all. We had to talk about Björn. She wanted to know what happened. I tried to explain, I tried to be truthful. She nodded and took down notes and mentioned something about a psych evaluation.

The hospital bed became my best friend for months. The four walls and the occasional nurse were great company. Three warm meals a day, medicine, TV and the occasional visit from Helen.

During her fifth visit, Helen said the police were considering adding more charges against me. She didn't elaborate. I desperately tried to pry the information from her, but she was a sealed vault. I could have strangled her, Gabriel offered to, I swatted away the joke and waited.

It was not long after that that Helen dropped in unexpectedly. My bad situation was about to get worse.

She sat like a china doll, polished and erect in the chair that she pulled closer to my bed. "The police are officially adding two murder chargers to your case," she said it as if she was discussing her sandwich options at the lunch counter.

I grabbed her hand. I could feel the heat drain from my body replaced by a cold searing panic. What other murder charges?

Helen snatched her hand away and gave me a look that ensured I understood touching her was off limits. I flinched back and pulled my knees into my chest, gathering strength to ask the questions I didn't really want the answer to.

"Who?" My voice was scratched and weak. I cleared my throat and tried again. "Who do they think I killed?"

She gave me a long look. Gauging me, testing me, wondering if she could trust me. I realised right then, she thought I was guilty, just like everyone else, guilty and a liar. And whatever new charges these were, I was fucked.

She pulled out some papers from her briefcase and continued in her monotonous tone. "You are being charged with the murder of Leon Edwards and Barry Thompson Junior."

If it wasn't for the shock wave that rushed through my body, I may have found a moment to laugh at Barry. Junior. He would have hated that. I could have tormented him with it forever.

"What are you talking about?" I found my voice pushing it through chattering teeth.

"Leon Edward's death was not an accident. With new evidence, it seems they now have enough to tie you in with his untimely death."

"Leon?" she looked at me as if I was a stupid kid, and

she was the exasperated teacher that would now have to explain it all again - but slowly. "But they said Marco did it."

"The investigation took a turn."

The hot tear that rolled along my cheek burned in the cold room. "But I loved him, I would never hurt him."

I could see her pursed lips pull tighter against her mouth, her eyes twitched at the corners, forced to remain in place. Her silent thoughts spewed all over my bed.

I loved Björn too.

I sucked in a snotty snivel and tried to keep my world from falling apart completely. "And Barry? What could they possibly think I did to Barry? He just disappeared."

"Barry Thomson's body was found in a number of pieces in the basement of 47 Main street. I believe it was your residence between 2003-2004?"

"Yes, but –"

"The basement flooded two weeks ago. The thawing snow caused a blockage in the pipe and it burst flooding the basement. Building maintenance found what was believed to be a human skeleton. Among the dismembered body they found a wallet and a cell phone. The ID belonged to Mr. Barry Thompson Junior. DNA tests will confirm his identity by week's end."

"So why are they blaming me? There's no evidence."

"Look Jane," she cut me off with another sharp lashing of her tongue. "I'm going to be honest with you, because believe it or not, I do want to help you, even if you don't want to help yourself."

My mouth dropped in an effort to talk, but she raised her hand to silence me.

"You, are what we in the industry call fucked." She didn't mince her words. "You were found in your home with Mr Hellström's body, the weapon and DNA evidence in just about every room of your apartment. New evidence has emerged of your whereabouts the night that Leon died, and Barry's death has produced questions that lead to you."

She sighed and straightened up as if embarrassed that she showed an ounce of humanity. "Our only defence, your only defence, is to plead insanity."

"What?" my voice faltered even as my body began to shake.

"Look Jane." There was her teacher to a stupid kid again. "When they found you, you insisted that Gabriel did it." Her eyebrows rose in both question and accusation. "And more than a few people have heard you mention his name, but Jane, you do realise he is a fictional character, don't you? He isn't real?"

I let her words sink in even as he sat on the edge of the bed and gave me an innocent look. I ignored him, the hot anger battling the sinking fear. He did this, all of this, and they think it was me.

Helen packed her papers into her case and stood up. "We will set up another meeting once you are released from hospital and we can talk about strategy. It seems that you will be released in the next few days. You will be taken from here to the local police station and be booked. Then they will take you downstairs where you will be put in a cell. Make sure you inform me and we can get proceedings ready for your bail." She waited just long enough to let me murmur or nod then turned around and left the room.

When the door closed behind her, I shot Gabriel a seething look. "You hurt them? It was you?"

"Don't you remember?"

"What are you talking about?"

"You know what I am talking about Jane. Search your memories. Who am I? Who are you?"

"I want you to leave."

"Jane." He took a step toward the bed.

"Leave Gabriel, I don't want to see you."

"Jane. Janey, I did this all for you, for us."

"No."

"I love you."

"Go away."

"Jane."

"JUST LEAVE." I must have screamed it because the door flew open and the guard burst into the room.

"What's going on here?" he looked at me suspicion clouding his features.

"Nothing." I fell back into the bed scanning the room. Gabriel was gone.

I pulled the cover over my head while the officer scoured the room. When he had discovered no one, he walked out reminding me to keep it down.

Neither Gabriel nor Helen returned after their last visit. The oppressive hospital room became smaller, the walls pushed against me as I was confined to the bed. My body ached and wrists screamed with discomfort while I was bound to the bed. All I wanted to do was get out, get up, be done with it all.

The end was coming. I just didn't know how fast.

The fresh air was cool and tinged with regret. The taller of the two policemen that had been watching over me, wheeled me out to the car park. The light of morning was almost too bright, and I sheltered my eyes. The wheelchair came to as top in front of an unmarked police car. The barrel-shaped officer held my door open and I climbed in, he indicated that I should fasten my seat belt and I obliged. It was a new sensation not having my wrists bound. I followed every instruction and order just to retain the use of my hands. The door slammed and the car shook as the two men climbed into their seats.

The police car smelled like burned cigarettes and vomit. I fought the urge to gag despite the bile rising in my throat. The two men in the front spoke about me as if I wasn't even there, I heard the word crazy and batshit floating around while my head lolled against the window taking in the cityscape as we neared the police station.

The day blurred into long corridors and slamming cell doors, into Clarice's panicked voice and Helen's unphased one, into cold bare walls and clanging metal.

My bail was served and paid for and for a moment I was free again. But not really. chains of grief and fear clung to my heart and weighed me down.

I was allowed to return home. It didn't feel like my home anymore.

Yellow crime scene tape stuck to my door leering at me. I pushed past it and scoured my apartment. My stomach coiled at the scene. Black fingertip marks were smeared on almost every surface, the floor was scuffed and scattered with overturned furniture, and dried black blood pooled in spots along my floor.

Was it mine? Was it Gabriel's? Was it...? I didn't want to think of his name.

I switched on my computer and emailed Clarice, she had been waiting patiently. I sent her the final book in the Guarding Gabriel series. It was my best work, epic, thrilling, heart wrenching, tear jerking finale. I knew the fans would love it. I turned my computer off, hoping it wasn't for the last time and gathered a few possessions. Clothes, some books, my toothbrush. I wasn't coming back. As I stepped towards the elevator, I suddenly felt like the same Jane that met Girsh on that rainy morning. Alone, with no home and a box full of a few possessions. I held the tears that welled in my eyes long enough to make it to Helen's waiting car. As we pulled away, I didn't look back.

I walked the media gauntlet on the way in to court. Despite all the police's 'efforts,' the media managed to find me at the back 'secret entrance'. They had labelled me the Fallen Angel. Probably had something to do with Gabriel's name. I shielded my face from the bright flashes that dazzled me as strong arms pulled me along to the safety of a closed door.

It wasn't the trial of the century, but, with Clarice, the old fox timed my latest release with the start of my court case. Book sales went berserk. Not only did the first print run almost sell out globally in a week, but readers were buying the very first book of the series. Guarding Gabriel was suddenly flying off the shelves. Despite their resentments, the publishing house was suddenly very happy with me again.

The courtroom was packed as the prosecution began their case against me. To them I was a piece of cloth, and strand by strand they were going to unravel me.

They started with Björn. Dissecting and gauging our relationship in front of everyone. Taking something beautiful and pure and dirtying it with ugly words.

The list of witnesses was long. An endless line-up of officers and experts. Each, in turn, they pointed fingers at me and described how they found me that night, the blood, the knife the screaming. They used words like trajectory and blood splatter, incoherent babble and Gabriel. Why did they use his name?

I didn't want to listen. Instead, I watched him watching me.

Gabriel.

He leaned in the far corner. His dark eyes resting on me. He didn't come close and I didn't want him to, but every day as I sat shrinking into my chair, I could feel his anger grow dimmer. Though I didn't want to admit that I needed him, he was my only friend.

Their final witness for Björn's case was Maja, his twin sister.

When she walked into the courtroom I gasped. The resemblance obvious and painful, but where Björn's eyes looked at me with desire and love, her ice-cold hatred froze me in my seat. She was his equal in every way. Her powerful stride and intelligent words, the way she flicked her hair in the same way he used to, and how her accent rolled in the same melodic way that his did. I wondered if she was as strong as him in bed too. Would she bite my nipples as hard or taste my wet pussy? I wondered what it would feel like to touch her soft skin and run my hands through her hair. If only she didn't look at me with so much loathing, I might have asked her to come home with me, to look at her, talk to her, feel her. To remind me of him.

When she finished her testimony, she stormed out and didn't give me a backwards glance.

In its third week, the trail seemed to be dragging forever. I had moved into a hotel room unable to live in my apartment. Björn covered every surface of it, figuratively and literally. The hotel room was near the courtroom. I stood at the window relishing the cold city air and trickles of city noise that filtered through the window. I was lonely. How had I fallen so far? So fast? My eyes fell on the giant billboard overhanging the highway. Even from this distance, I could see Gabriel's perfect face glowing at me. He smirked at me even as he held Mia.

The week that they started talking about Leon I fished out the red lingerie he had given me. I wore it every day. It was like feeling his hands on me. Like he was right there with me. Gabriel sat across the courtroom from me, always smiling, always supportive, sometimes he would even hold my hand as I cried through the terrible things they said. None of that was true.

Another group of experts gave testimonies. My mouth hung open as they produced evidence and proof of my alleged misdeeds.

Despite all their accusations, I loved Leon. I would have never cut the brakes in his car. I had no knowledge of cars or how they work.

The witnesses presented my research history. Searches that had been wiped from my computer's memory and were recovered by the forensic team. I had no recollection of these. Helen did her best to dispute facts, I was a writer after all, but facts *were* facts, and despite her prestigious law degree, being a writer didn't seem to float as a defence.

When Scott came to court, he glared at me with angry disappointed eyes. A contrast to the sad, needy eyes at his brother's funeral. His anger made him seem bigger, broader, unruly, almost attractive. Maybe that's what he was always missing, some fucking emotion. He didn't testify, we hadn't really spoken in years, but Sammy did.

My stomach rolled as she sauntered into the courtroom. Even in a full body suit, she could command everyone's attention. I tried to catch her eye implore her to think of what she was doing and why, but she didn't look at me. Not even once.

That hurt more than the seething, angry looks I had received up until then. It was a cold knife in my heart all over again.

Sammy's testimony was short. She spoke of our single phone call, the one where she told me about Leon. The one when I pushed Gabriel away. The one that crushed my soul, and here she was all over again ripping that wound open, and mocking my grief by telling the world I was talking to an imaginary man.

My heart cracked a little more, the wedge piercing it constructed of anger and disappointment.

Barry was the hardest. Not because I loved him or he meant anything to me. We never got there, never got a chance to see what we might have been. It was just too graphic, too disturbing. Too unbelievable.

But possibly worse, it was the horrified look in the jury's eyes. The disbelief. How they bought everything the investigators fed them.

The so-called experts were back explaining how I had dismembered him and hidden him in the basement. How in a luminol test of number 19, blood had been found, pooled and smeared on my walls. How I had destroyed his phone, and how in a final act of cruelty I shoved a butt plug in his ass.

I wish I could have stood up and screamed at them to just look at me. How could they see me as this murderess that carried body parts down to the basement? At some stage, I would tell them Barry enjoyed the butt plug up his ass, but I think everyone stopped listening by then.

Despite the gore, and ugliness of the weeks that fell into one another in endless talks and testimonies, Grish was always there. A solemn quiet figure in the back. A sentinel of stoic support. Non-judgemental and worried, like a father who is deeply disappointed but wants to tell their kids he would be there no matter what.

I was his no matter what.

Until Rebecca.

Rebecca.

It took me a long moment to remember her mousy face. The last time I saw it, it had a dick in its mouth.

Josh's dick.

On that day, her hair wasn't wound tight into a serious bun and her body wasn't covered in a thick body tight sweater. Josh's fingers were twisted in her hair, it was clumped around her face with sweat, her boobs bounced up and down slapping against one another, as Josh's hand guided her head while she sucked him off.

What the fuck was she doing here?

"State your full name for the record." The scrawny balding prosecutor smiled at her. I wondered if maybe she sucked his cock too.

"Rebecca Bradshaw."

"Rebecca." The prosecutor's voice sounded whiny. "How do you know the defendant?"

"I don't really know her."

"Oh?" a theatrical sound followed by extreme over-exaggerated eyebrow raise. "Well would you like to tell the court how you know the defendant?"

"We dated the same man."

I gaffed. Dated. She fucked my boyfriend. A murmur went up in the court and died down.

"What was his name?"

"Josh Rogers."

"And how did you meet Mr. Rogers?"

"At a club one night. We were both drinking alone, he came over and we started talking."

"And then?"

"And then we got on so well that we met a number of other times."

"And were you aware that he was in a relationship with another woman?"

"Not at first, but after a while, yes." Biatch! I smiled in victory as the court burst into another judgemental murmur.

"Could you tell the court how you found out about her?"

"He told me."

"And you chose to remain with this man?"

"Yes." She squared her shoulders as if daring anyone to question her decision to sleep with a man in a relationship. For once, all eyes were not on me.

"Did he end things with her?"

"No. She caught us together."

I could feel that she was not going to give more detail and that the prosecutor would sail right over the finer details.

"You were sucking his cock on your knees," I shouted at her as the court erupted into laughter and talk. Her face became the colour of ripe strawberries and the judge smashed his gavel on its wooden disc threatening to throw me out should I open my mouth again. There was no need. I did what I needed to do.

"So," the prosecutor tried to salvage his witness. "You were in a sexual relationship with Mr. Rogers?"

Rebecca cleared her throat. "Yes."

"What happened after she caught you together?"

"She lost her shit completely. She started yelling and throwing things, smashing all his stuff. She went completely insane."

"Did she threaten you?"

"She threatened Josh. She told him he better not leave her. She reminded him that he told her that he loved her," Rebecca sniggered. "She turned into a snivelling pathetic mess. Josh was pissed. He tried to break up with her a few times, but she always turned into a manipulative little girl that guilted him into staying." My mouth twitched as I tried to set her alight with my eyes. Lies!

"He promised me that he would get rid of her, so maybe the fact she caught us together was a blessing in disguise, the push she needed to set him free."

"Tell us what happened next."

"He told me to leave. He promised he would sort things out with her, and that we would be together after."

"Is that what happened?"

"No."

"What did happen then Miss. Bradshaw?"

"Josh called me a few hours later. He said that he and Alison had broken up and that he wanted to meet up the following day to pick up where we left off." Her cheeks burned bright pink.

"Miss Bradshaw, who is Alison?"

"That woman over there." She pointed right at me. "When Josh was dating her, she was going by Alison Wynters."

The courtroom erupted for a third time. I could feel all eyes shift to me. I didn't see the big deal, people changed names all the time.

"Miss Bradshaw, did you meet Josh the next day?"

"No."

"No?"

"No."

I rolled my eyes. She said no already. Move on.

"Tell us what happened."

"He disappeared." Another low murmur, but this time there was tension, anticipation, I could almost hear the crowd in the court slide to the edge of their seats.

"What do you mean?"

"He didn't call me the next day, or the day after that. I went to his apartment and knocked. He didn't answer. I got his spare key and went inside. Most of the stuff from the night she caught us was cleaned up. Some of his clothes were missing, his favourite Led Zeppelin singlet and some other metal shirts, also a tie-dyed blue and purple sheet that he had as a wall hanging, but that was it, the rest of his stuff was left behind. His phone and wallet were gone."

"That's a very specific inventory, did you spend much time going through his stuff?"

"I didn't need to, these shirts were hung in a display rack, it was his concert collection, merch he had bought or clothes he wore only for concerts, they were ripped from moshing and dirty from mud, and stank of beer, he never washed them, it was his pride and joy. It was disgusting if you ask me, but I guess it was his thing."

I could feel the air snap as she mentioned the sheet, the shirt, the specifics. From the corner of my eye, I saw Grish as he stood and slunk away silently from the courtroom. That was the last time I saw him. Maybe some wounds are too hard to heal and maybe I had cut him too deeply.

His absence left a sharp shard of regret in my gut, whose edges, I can only hope, will dull with time. I grieve for him, but it is worse than grieving for the dead, for they can never forgive, and he has chosen not to.

"So, he left you?"

"No."

"So, what did happen Miss Bradshaw?"

"He never came back. You don't just leave everything behind and not come back. I called the police, they investigated and he ended up on the missing person's register. He's never been found."

"And you suspect Miss Miller had something to do with his disappearance?"

Helen shot out of her chair her voice harsh, "Objection, speculation. She is not a qualified detective."

"I'll allow the witness to answer."

"Your honour, we are not here to find out what the witness thinks, only what she knows."

"Your objection has been noted. Now sit down Miss Ying."

Helen sat down stiffly her expression as unreadable as ever.

"Miss Bradshaw?" the prosecutor nudged.

"I think she killed him and hid him somewhere, just like she did with all these other men."

"Did you go to the police with your worries?"

"I did."

"What did they say?"

"That there was no such person as Alison Wynters and therefore they could not investigate her, nor could they find her. Now we know why."

"Indeed Miss Bradshaw, thank you. That will be all."

Helen stood up, stiff and agitated.

"Miss Bradshaw, has a body been found?"

"No."

"Is there any concrete proof that Josh is dead?"

"No, But –"

"Did the police treat his disappearance as suspicious?"

"No, but –"

"So, there is a possibility that he is alive, and he just left you and you are looking for someone to blame?"

"No, he didn't leave me, he –"

"Is there a possibility that he is alive Miss Bradshaw?"

She looked to the prosecutor suddenly a lost little lamb.

"Yes, I guess that's possible, but –"

"No further questions your honour."

Helen sat down just as stiffly as she stood up, but I could see the edge of a suppressed, satisfied smile along her rigid mouth and tight eyes. If she wasn't such a stiff, I would have given her a high five.

Take that Rebecca.

That's what you get for sucking my boyfriend's dick.

Later that day, Helen asked me if she had to worry about another body surfacing. I assured her I knew nothing of Josh's whereabouts or disappearance. When she asked me if Alison did, I scowled at her. She didn't bring it up again.

Not for two weeks anyway.

It took the police two weeks to find Josh. He wasn't alive. They never did tie me to his murder, but the suspicion was always there, hanging like a dark cloud above my head, like a noose around my neck. Despite Helen's best efforts, the jury heard the rumours, the details, as they were accidentally leaked. The damage was done.

The prosecution's case ended, and then it was Helen's turn to try and dig me out from beneath the steaming pile of crap I was buried under.

My trial lasted eight weeks. I had to wait ten days for the jury to come back, which in all honesty was a surprise. I still don't know why they took so long.

When they found me guilty, my heart jolted, my legs turned to jelly and if it wasn't for Gabriel holding me up, I would have fallen. My life fractured like an iced river at the beginning of spring.

"How could this happen?" I grabbed Helen who snatched her hand away.

"For your sake, I hope they bought our defence."

It was all the reassurance she gave me. I glared at her through wounded tearful eyes.

The judge said we would reconvene in the morning for sentencing.

That night was one of the longest in my life. The hotel room felt small, trapping me within its walls. I wanted to go walking, running, flying. I wanted to disappear into the ether and be one with the world. I was scared. And I was alone. Until I wasn't.

I felt him before I saw him, like a familiar smell or memory. He was there. Sitting on the couch.

"What are you doing here?" I didn't turn to him.

"I miss you Jane." His voice sounded small, remorseful.

I turned to him. "You're not supposed to be here anymore."

He rose to from the couch and closed the distance between us.

I took a backwards step just to find my back against the wall. "We need each other Jane."

He stood inches from me, his towering height too close and too hot. His eyes implored mine. "Jane." It was a plea on his lips.

Gabriel lifted a finger and traced the jagged scar on my chest. "I'm not going anywhere, Jane, not until you forgive me."

I pulled at his shirt, the buttons falling away to reveal the rough scar along his bare muscular chest.

"Did you do all those terrible things they said I did?" I looked into Gabriel's eyes.

"For you."

"But why?"

"Because they said they loved you."

"They did! They all did! They promised."

"Just like your parents did when they left you with him? Just like he did? When he came in the dark with his heavy hands and stinking breath? *He* told you he loved you."

"Stop!"

"I did it for us, for you."

"Gabriel." I traced my fingers over the thick wounded flesh on his chest, leaning in, I kissed the ugly mark. I heard the low growl in his throat. I breathed him in. Spice and sweat and need. He smelled like home, my home. "I feel so broken, you've cut me to the very core."

"And I can fix you from the inside out. If we are going to survive this, we have to forgive each other. Let me love you."

"Love me?"

"Always."

"Gabriel." I choked on his name. "I forgive you." And I did. He knew what was best for me. He always had.

The nurse switched the light off as she left my room. The medicine was about to kick in. The room grew soft, the world was beautiful. I had to hurry if I wanted to see him, the pills always made him fuzzy.

I turned my head on my pillow and smiled at Gabriel who smiled back, only love in his eyes.

His fingers brushed my cheek, "I will never leave you Jane, we're going to be together forever."

THE END

ACKNOWLEDGMENTS

I would like to start by thanking you, the reader, for taking the time to pick up this book, from an unknown, and giving it a chance. I hope that it exceeded your expectations and that you will enjoy this journey with me in the future.

I would love to thank my wonderful friend and beta reader, Dawn. Her enthusiasm knows no boundaries, her genuine love for books, reading, and helping authors is contagious and humbling. I have loved having her in my corner. Thank you.

To all my other betas and C/Ps, your input and critiques have been invaluable. Without you, Gabriel would not have been where he is today.

To my family, without whom this book would have been finished months ago.

To all the Gabriels out there that keep us up at night.

ABOUT THE AUTHOR

Jane Wynters doesn't quite know how to answer the question of "where are you from?" She's moved from place to place like a snowflake on the wind always searching for a safe place to land. She loves meeting new people and exploring new places. She loves reading, writing and conjuring new worlds from her imagination.

facebook.com/J-A-Wynters-Author-1246599972167001

instagram.com/jane_wynters_author

amazon.com/author/jawynters

bookbub.com/profile/j-a-wynters

goodreads.com/JAWynters

ALSO BY J. A. WYNTERS

Coming soon:

Gabriel Book 1

Why not leave a review and tell others how much you loved
Guarding Gabriel?

Guarding Gabriel